THE PENNYPACKERS GO ON VACATION

ALSO BY LISA DOAN

Chadwick's Epic Revenge
The Berenson Schemes series
The Alarming Career of Sir Richard Blackstone

THE
PENNYPACKERS
GO ON
VACATION

Lisa Doan

Illustrated by Marta Kissi

Roaring Brook Press
New York City

Text copyright © 2019 by Lisa Doan
Illustrations copyright © 2019 by Marta Kissi
Published by Roaring Brook Press
Roaring Brook Press is a division of
Holtzbrinck Publishing Holdings Limited Partnership
175 Fifth Avenue, New York, NY 10010
mackids.com

Library of Congress Control Number: 2018956034

ISBN: 978-1-250-15411-8

Our books may be purchased in bulk for promotional, educational, or
business use. Please contact your local bookseller or the Macmillan Corporate
and Premium Sales Department at (800) 221-7945 ext. 5442 or by email at
MacmillanSpecialMarkets@macmillan.com.

First edition, 2019
Book design by Aimee Fleck
Printed in the United States of America by LSC Communications,
Harrisonburg, Virginia

1 3 5 7 9 10 8 6 4 2

For Betty Ann Doan

Chapter One

Engines roaring, Frontier Airlines Flight 1001 barreled down the runway. Charlie Pennypacker gripped the armrests—he was finally going somewhere.

He'd spent years harassing his dad to take them on a trip. He'd lobbied for surfing the twenty-one-foot waves of Teahupo'o in Tahiti or bungee jumping into the Villarrica Volcano in Chile. Or how about rafting the rapids of the Amazon basin or hiking up Machu Picchu?

After he'd been laughed out of the living room over those ideas, he'd suggested hiking down the Grand Canyon or even camping in Yellowstone.

He'd finally been reduced to proposing an off-season weekend at a low-budget Jersey Shore motel.

But even the cheapest motel in New Jersey was too rich

for Mr. Pennypacker's blood. He grudgingly allowed cash to be peeled out of his tightfisted grip for absolute necessities, but his list of what was necessary was short and his ideas about what should be paid was low. As Mr. Pennypacker often said, "Throw perfectly good money at a vacation and what have you got? Just memories, which don't increase in value, can't be re-sold, and will fly right out of your head the minute you get dementia!"

On the occasions that cash *had* somehow been ripped out of Mr. Pennypacker's hands, he was not a gracious loser. Months ago, Mrs. Pennypacker noticed Charlie had outgrown all his pants and bought him six new pairs. When Charlie got back from the mall, Mr. Pennypacker had eyed his legs like they were regular Benedict Arnolds and loudly wondered about exactly how many growth spurts were in the works.

To meet his son halfway in his outrageous demands for a vacation, Mr. Pennypacker had taken to staging them in the backyard. Backyard vacations were free, and no airline, bus line, restaurant, tour guide, hotel, or motel insisted on being paid.

The summer before, the Pennypackers had camped under their oak tree, imagining they were in the Maine woods. According to his dad, it was exactly like Maine, except without the ticks, the hunters who would accidentally shoot you dead, or the bears who would tear you apart if the hunters didn't get you first.

But now the Pennypackers were on their way to an island-hopping adventure in the heart of the Caribbean. The *real* Caribbean, not a fake one in the backyard.

Charlie leaned his head against the plane's window as Philadelphia's skyline faded into the distance. Three weeks ago, his dad had come home proudly waving a five-thousand-dollar check—a bonus for helping his accounting firm open a new office. Mr. Pennypacker wouldn't have waved that check around so enthusiastically if he'd known that his wife was secretly planning an off-property vacation.

Mrs. Pennypacker, a lawyer with mad skills at arguing her points, had her own ideas about money. She waged daring bidding wars on eBay, had her hair and nails done in a high-end salon, and tipped generously. Now, it turned out, she wanted to throw even more money away on a vacation.

Peggy Pennypacker sharpened all her lawyerly arrows and fired off the sort of dark threats that made Mr. Pennypacker shiver. And sometimes cry.

"Charles, I will now begin my closing argument on the consequences of not spending the money on a family vacation.

From this day forward," she said, dramatically pointing one finger toward the ceiling, "I will run a hot shower and not even be in it. I will just watch gallons of expensive hot water go down the drain."

Charlie stood behind his dad and softly whispered, "Expensive water. Down drain."

Mr. Pennypacker flinched. He was violently against drains and anything expensive disappearing down them.

Mrs. Pennypacker clasped her hands behind her back and strolled in front of the kitchen counter. "Further, the next time a Nigerian potentate emails that he would be gracious enough to transfer five million dollars to our bank account, I will say, 'Get a pen, good sir, while I tell you all of our personal information.' Naturally, our accounts will be drained in under an hour."

"Accounts down drain, too," Charlie whispered. He gently blew at his dad's neck, hoping to create a shiver up his spine.

Mrs. Pennypacker noted with satisfaction that sweat droplets had erupted on her husband's forehead. A dramatic courtroom silence settled over the kitchen. "At this very moment," she said softly, "I am looking for matches to burn my special Pfeffernüsse cookie recipe, sent to me by my childhood Danish pen pal. If we vacation in the backyard one more

4

time, it will go up in a puff of smoke. You shall notice a flame springing up shortly."

"Pfeffernüsse," Charlie whispered. "Puff of smoke."

With the loss of Pfeffernüsse cookies on the horizon, Charlie's dad had crumpled to the linoleum, thereby resting his case in a heap of thrifty defeat. The jury was in—the Pennypackers were going on vacation.

Once Mr. Pennypacker had picked himself up off the floor and eaten a handful of animal crackers to restore his blood sugar, he suddenly got enthusiastic about the idea of a real vacation. He insisted he would handle all the arrangements and swore it would be a first-rate holiday.

Charlie had been suspicious of this new devil-may-care attitude. He assumed his dad would come up with the cheapest road trip possible. He figured they'd hop on their bikes, have shepherd's pie at the Irish pub, and pretend they were biking across the Emerald Isle. Or maybe they'd rope a pagoda to the top of the car, order shredded pork at the Wok This Way, and pretend they were exploring China's Hunan Province.

Even when they went to get passports, Charlie hadn't been convinced they would really go somewhere. He thought it might be some kind of ruse, like the time they had driven through the parking lot of Trop Cher, a five-star French restaurant, and then somehow ended up with chalupas at Taco Bell.

But then came the miracle. His dad told Olive they were booked on a Disney cruise. A person would have to be mad as a hatter to mess with six-year-old Olive Pennypacker when it came to Disney. Every day, Olive sat cross-legged in front of the television like a sentry guarding a castle, mesmerized by Mickey Mouse Clubhouse or Puppy Dog Pals or that adorable scamp of a bloodsucker, Vampirina. There might be other, stronger people in the house, but Olive would fight for the remote with the fearlessness and aggression of an enraged honey badger.

If Mr. Pennypacker had told the enraged honey badger that they were going on a Disney cruise, then it was true. They were actually going on a real vacation. And not just any vacation! A top-of-the-line, first-rate, all-you-could-eat, luxury, living-like-a-billionaire, childhood-fever-dream Caribbean cruise.

As the plane rose over the clouds, Charlie relaxed his grip on the armrests. The danger of Mr. Pennypacker changing his mind, turning the plane around, and demanding his money back had passed.

He glanced over at his sister. Olive's new dress, as adorable as his mom claimed it was, did nothing to hide the black hole in her mouth caused by her missing front teeth. As soon as any of her baby teeth came loose, she ripped them out of her gums with gusto. Her tributes to the Tooth Fairy were frightening, and the last had ended with blood splatter on the living room rug. Charlie assumed that when she ran out of baby teeth, she'd start working on her permanent teeth. Since her mouth had no front gate, fine sprays of spit flew out when she talked. The woman across the aisle had made the mistake of telling Olive her name. (It was Marjorie.) Olive had been talking and spitting at Marjorie ever since.

"Cinderella will like me better than my friend Carrie," Olive said, with a particularly generous spit. "Carrie is my best friend and she met Cinderella at Disney World, but Carrie is not as good as me. It's not *my* fault that I'm better! Do you have a friend? Are you better than them?"

Charlie wondered if he should tell Olive to stop talking, but then he decided that was Marjorie's problem. He leaned his head against the window and imagined cruising on a luxury ocean liner. During the day, he planned to swim in the Olympic-sized pool and take breaks by flying down a waterslide. He didn't know which ship they were on, his dad said that was a surprise, but Charlie had high hopes that he would find himself climbing the steps to an AquaDuck—half water slide, half rollercoaster, and total madness.

After a full day of twists, turns, and stomach-churning drops, he would head to the food buffets. He would drink gallons of orange soda accompanied by shrimp, a seafood delicacy that had never crossed the threshold of the Pennypacker household. His dad said that one shrimp was affordable, but you had to eat at least six, and that's where *they* got you on the price. (*They* featured prominently in Mr. Pennypacker's theories—Charlie envisioned a cabal of old men sitting around a boardroom, dreaming up plots on how to ruin people's lives by getting them, usually on the price.)

After exhausting himself on the AquaDuck, drinking unlimited soda, and eating expensive shrimp, Charlie could go back to school with something real to talk about. Not like last year when he'd described camping in the Maine woods and Gunter Hwang had said, "So now it's the Maine woods in your backyard? I thought your backyard was supposed to be sunny Spain. Oh never mind, that was the summer before."

He'd had to jump on Gunter and throw him to the ground in some kind of last-ditch effort to save his reputation. That had led to a formal apology delivered in the principal's office, an essay titled "Why It's Wrong to Tackle People," and two weeks of detention.

Gunter Hwang, ex-best friend, lived next door to the Pennypackers. Every time Charlie's dad tricked out the backyard for some imaginary trip, Gunter leaned out his bedroom window and gave Charlie's dad the thumbs-up while scribbling notes and snapping photos to be shared on social media. Gunter liked to post Charlie's backyard vacations next to his own trips overseas to visit his mom's family in Germany or his dad's family in South Korea. He made a point of strutting around in the T-shirts he bought, like I HEART BERLIN and SEOUL HAS SOUL and one especially annoying one that said MR. WORLDWIDE. In case Charlie didn't get the message about all his stupid T-shirts, Gunter had once said to him:

"The message is, I actually go places, and you vacation in the backyard."

To be sure that Gunter knew he had actually gone somewhere, Charlie had left a note taped to the mailbox, printed out in a fancy font so it would look like an expensive announcement.

The Pennypacker family will be Disney cruising until the 27th in a stateroom on a luxury cruise ship that is over a thousand feet long and will carry hundreds of other extravagant passengers except for Gunter Hwang.

To be totally sure Gunter would see it, he'd run to the backyard picnic table and used Olive's sidewalk chalk to write on it in large letters: *CHECK THE MAILBOX.*

Though he wrote that the Pennypackers would be vacationing in a stateroom, Charlie did not believe his dad would have splurged for that kind of luxury. Especially since Mr. Pennypacker had just told the flight attendant that if the family was thirsty they could drink water right out of the bathroom sink and let's see how Frontier Airlines figures out how to charge him for it.

Charlie was actually a little concerned about how far his dad might have gone to save a few dollars. What if he'd made some kind of deal and they would stay in dank rooms next to the ship's engines? He could already hear his dad saying, "So what? You can't even see your room when you're sleeping. The joke is on the clowns who paid for rooms they can't even see!"

Still, Gunter Hwang would never know that Charlie had slept next to the engines. Gunter would see his stylish announcement taped to the mailbox, grab his phone, and look up Disney Cruise Line's website. The first thing he'd see would be a picture of an elegant stateroom. Then Gunter, consumed with rage and envy, would throw his phone on the ground. Let Monsieur Hwang report *that* at school.

. . .

The Miami airport teemed with people racing up and down long hallways, all hurrying to a thousand different destinations. Charlie had guessed his family were the only people that vacationed in the backyard—suspicion confirmed.

They stood at the baggage carousel for ages, watching other

people's bags roll past them, while Olive cried, "Where is it? Where is Hello Kitty? Where?"

Finally, they got their bags, including the freakishly pink Hello Kitty, and made their way to the doors. A tall man, whose arms and legs were rail thin, but whose stomach stuck out so perfectly round that it looked like a set of twins were preparing to fight their way out, held up a sign that read: THE PENNYPACKERS, PARTY OF FOUR.

It was like they were celebrities.

Mr. Pennypacker waved. The man with the sign ambled over to them. "Hello, Pennypackers," he said in a booming voice. "I'm Ignatius Wisner, your captain. Follow me, folks!"

The captain. The captain of the ship had come personally. This was what it was like to be a high roller, living large and roaming around the globe.

The doors swung open, and the heat hit Charlie like a wall of hot, thick soup. The Florida sunshine was blinding, and he could feel it burning the top of his head.

"Here we are. Hop in," Captain Wisner said, slapping a navy-colored hat with a white brim on his head.

They stood in front of a black van with its doors open. Charlie was surprised that it didn't have the Disney logo on it, but that it did have dents, peeling paint, a rearview mirror attached with duct tape, and a bumper tied on with rope. It looked like the kind of vehicle that somebody would report to the police if it was parked outside a school.

His mom took it all in and then looked coolly at her husband. Mr. Pennypacker dove into the van.

"Where's Mickey?" Olive demanded, climbing in after Mr. Pennypacker and throwing Hello Kitty facedown on the floor.

"He's already on board, miss," Ignatius Wisner said, helping Mrs. Pennypacker and Charlie get in. "Lots of things to do before our departure, you see. He is a busy, busy mouse."

"Is Minnie helping him?" Olive asked.

Captain Wisner tipped his hat to Olive and closed the van door without answering her. Charlie presumed this was because he didn't yet know that she was the Question Viking— relentless and savage in her hunt for answers.

The captain hopped into the driver's seat and turned the key. The engine sputtered, then died, sputtered again and died. Just when Charlie became convinced it had gone on strike, it fired up.

"Hey, you!" Olive said, leaning forward toward the captain. "I said, is Minnie helping Mickey with all the work he has to do?"

Mrs. Pennypacker laid a hand on Olive's arm and said quietly, "Nobody's name is 'hey you.' Apologize, madam."

"Sorry and is Minnie helping Mickey?" Olive said with grim determination.

"Um, sadly," Captain Wisner said from the driver's seat, "Mickey and Minnie broke up."

"What'ya mean they broke up?" Olive cried. "They can't break up, they're not allowed! They have to be together."

Though Charlie had outgrown Mickey and Minnie, he had to agree with Olive on that particular point. Since when did Disney characters break up?

"Don't you worry, little one," the captain said. "It won't last long. Some silly dust-up over pancakes can't keep them apart forever."

Now Mickey and Minnie were having arguments in front of people? About pancakes?

"Minnie better be there when I get there," Olive said, issuing the order as if she were a general of the armed forces. "I will tell her, I will say, 'Minnie, you make Mickey say he's sorry. If he won't, I will send him to his room to think about it.' And then . . ."

For the next twenty minutes, as they weaved in and out of traffic toward the port, spit flew in every direction as Olive advised Minnie on how to manage Mickey. When she ran out of orders, she lapsed into some sort of weird marriage counseling session. Olive felt that Minnie could just let Mickey think he's right because Minnie would always secretly know that he was WRONG. If that didn't work, Minnie could write a note in Mickey's handwriting that said, "I am WRONG" and then show him his own signed confession.

Charlie knew the signed confession gambit wouldn't work; Olive had already tried it and failed miserably. She'd eaten a whole family-sized bag of Doritos and left a note inside that said *Sharly did it*. Spelling Charlie's name wrong in purple crayon had been a tip-off that all was not as it seemed. The other tip-off had been the bag's location under Olive's bed.

Charlie looked over at his mom and dad to see what they thought about the Mickey and Minnie breakup. Mr. Pennypacker was doggedly gazing out the window and pointing out interesting landmarks, like the sign they had just passed that said a Quarter Pounder at McDonald's was just a quarter mile away.

Mrs. Pennypacker was staring at her husband with squinted eyes, like she was about to launch a courtroom interrogation.

Something was brewing.

When something was brewing between Charlie's mom and

dad, the cause was always money. Mr. Pennypacker was a demon with a vacuum, cooked most nights, kept the family calendar, and did most of the laundry. It was just money that got him in trouble.

The last major incident had involved the thermostat. All winter long, they had been freezing in their own home. They watched television under a big pile of blankets, jogged around the house to warm up, and hung around the stove when something was cooking. Mrs. Pennypacker finally called in a heating company. The nice gentleman from Hankin Heater Repair showed Mrs. Pennypacker how the thermostat had been tampered with, and how while it *said* sixty-eight, it was really set at fifty-eight. Mr. Pennypacker had come home that day to find himself in near-tropical conditions, his wife in shorts, and the new thermostat set to seventy-eight to make up for all the heat they hadn't used for months.

"Charles," Mrs. Pennypacker said softly, "if there's something I should know about this vacation, tell me now."

Mr. Pennypacker pointed out the window. "Look! There's a Burger King, too! They really have it all in Miami."

The van pulled into terminal J and they showed their passports to the security guards.

Mrs. Pennypacker continued to stare at her husband.

Mr. Pennypacker desperately searched for interesting land-marks to point out through the window, though he had run out of fast-food restaurants and had just been reduced to exclaiming, "That car looks exactly like our car at home!"

Mrs. Pennypacker dug into her purse and pulled out a pack of Trident cinnamon gum. The Trident was chewed for only two things—getting ready to demolish a defendant in court or getting ready to demolish a defendant in her family. "Indeed," she said, double-dosing herself with two pieces. "I suppose spotting a Honda Civic *is* rare. How many even exist? One? Two? Fifty million?"

"Folks," Ignatius Wisner said over his shoulder, "we have arrived."

Charlie looked around for the ship. There were cruise ships in the distance, moored at other docks. They were white and shining, ten stories high and a thousand feet long. At this dock, all he saw was a hundred-foot-long boat that had even more peeling paint than the van. Then he saw the logo on the bow.

Charlie leaned forward to get a look at his dad. "Wisney Cruises?" he asked. "You booked us on a Wisney cruise? What is that? That's not Disney."

"What'ya mean it's not Disney?" Olive said, whipping her head toward Charlie. "It better be Disney."

"It's practically exactly like Disney," Mr. Pennypacker said. "You won't even know the difference."

Chapter Two

"That is not a cruise ship," Charlie said, pointing. "It's just a big boat. Where's the Olympic-sized pool? Where's the AquaDuck? Is there even room in there for an elaborate food buffet? I was going to try shrimp."

Captain Wisner said, "That fine lady you see in front of you is the *Aladdin's Dream*. A more stalwart boat there never was. Don't you worry that she ain't as big as some others. She has heart, she does."

There was a long silence in the van as the occupants stared at the boat.

"Anyhow, folks," the captain continued, "what we got here is quality cruising. Sure, you could go on one of those behemoths over there, get a stomach flu, and wretch over your balcony for a week."

"That is so true!" Mr. Pennypacker said. "Everybody gets sick on those things."

"Then," the captain continued, "after you've staggered out of your cabin ten pounds lighter than when you started, you could get in line with five hundred other people just to get an ice cream cone. Not on my watch, folks. You want a cone, you probably got a cone, assuming we brought them on board in the first place."

"Who wants to wait in line for a cone?" Mr. Pennypacker asked. "I mean, who?"

"And as for the entertainment on those tin cans over there," the captain continued, "you just don't know what you'll get. One guy told me he paid thousands for his trip and only got a mime."

"A mime," Mr. Pennypacker said. "Who even likes mimes?"

"I don't like mimes, Mr. Pennypacker," the captain said. "An entertainer, in my humble opinion, should have something

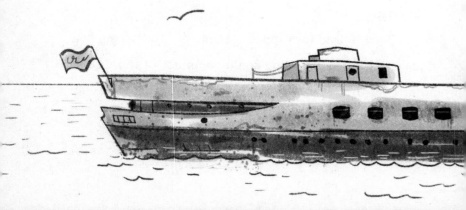

to *say* if you're gonna get your money's worth. No, on my ship, you're gonna have a personalized experience, cruising like you are royalty."

"Cruising like royalty," Mr. Pennypacker said. "That's how we roll."

Olive cried, "You better have Mickey and Minnie because if you don't, I'm going home."

"Now, Olive, don't worry about a thing," Mr. Pennypacker said. "You will be swamped with Disney-like characters. Every time you turn around one will be staring you in the face."

"I can't believe you did this," Charlie said. "What am I supposed to do all day with no pool and no AquaDuck?"

"Ah," Mr. Pennypacker said. "I've got you covered, Charlie. Your friend Gunter is coming along."

"Gunter?" Charlie asked. "Gunter Hwang?" A feeling of dread crept up his back like a slimy and slow-moving slug.

"Mr. Hwang was the one who tipped me off to this fantastic cruise line in the first place," Mr. Pennypacker said, avoiding Charlie's eye. "Good guy, Mr. Hwang."

"Gunter Hwang is my sworn enemy," Charlie said.

"Among all the other things you didn't tell me," Mrs. Pennypacker said, "like the difference between Disney and Disney-like, you certainly didn't mention that our neighbors were joining us."

"Now, I know you're a little cool on Gunter's mom," Mr. Pennypacker said, "on account of her trying to copy your Pfeffernüsse cookie recipe for the school bake sale that time, but she's not even coming. It was only Gunter's dad that had planned to come."

"Had planned to come?" Mrs. Pennypacker asked. "What do you mean by *had* planned?"

"Well, that would be, for one thing," Mr. Pennypacker stuttered, "mostly because Gunter's dad can't make it. Unexpected, last minute, unforeseen, surprise business trip—the worst kind, in my opinion. They should probably be against the law. Anyhoo, I said, being the gracious neighbor that I am, that Gunter could come with us. Those two went off to Key West for a few days, and then he's putting Gunter on a plane here, while *he* gets on a plane to Houston for that danged unforeseen trip. Houston! Can you imagine? How hot is Houston in the summer? Who even goes to Houston?"

"Wait," Mrs. Pennypacker said, chewing gum like a jackhammer. "Now we're babysitting?"

"Is Gunter really a baby?" Mr. Pennypacker asked. "He's the same age as Charlie."

"Hold on a minute," Charlie said. "You know Gunter Hwang is not my friend anymore, and you could care less about being a gracious neighbor. You complained when we had Missy Campbell spend the night while her mom was in the hospital having a baby. You said she was eating us out of house and home after she asked for a second bowl of cereal. So why, all of a sudden, would you bring Gunter on our vacation?"

"Yes, Charles," Mrs. Pennypacker said. "Why *is* Gunter coming with us? And think carefully before you answer. I want the absolute truth as if you were in a court of law."

Mr. Pennypacker closed his eyes, seeming to consider exactly how absolute or not absolute a truth he might safely shoot for in court. As usual, he couldn't hold up against his wife's lawyerly stare for long. He slumped and whispered, "Gunter's dad is paying me thirty dollars a day."

And there it was. Mr. Pennypacker had sold out their

family vacation for a Disney-*like* cruise and thirty dollars a day.

Mrs. Pennypacker let out a long, slow breath. It was the kind of breath she took when she realized that Mr. Pennypacker had replaced all their dinner plates with slightly smaller plates to give the family the illusion that they were eating more than they really were. It was the kind of breath she took when her husband fainted after discovering how much Olive's Hello Kitty backpack had cost, due to an ill-advised bidding war on eBay.

"I suppose," she said quietly, "we had better make the best of it."

"That's the spirit!" Mr. Pennypacker said.

Charlie stared at his dad. Gunter Hwang was going on his vacation. Gunter would see exactly what kind of vacation it was. Had he read the note on the mailbox? Charlie could already envision the first day of school. Gunter would lean over his desk and say, "A Disney-*like* cruise, was it?"

"So not only," Charlie said, "is our trip wrecked, but Dad decided to bring Gunter Hwang along for thirty dollars a day, which means the whole school will find out about it. It's another Pennypacker vacation fiasco."

"Well, I hardly think it's a fiasco . . . ," Mr. Pennypacker trailed off as if he could not pinpoint the exact word that would better describe the situation.

"Folks," Captain Wisner said, "family drama is nothing if not fascinating. On the other hand, it tends to be fascinating only to the family involved. I've got one more airport run to make, so let's get you on board."

"I say when we go!" Olive shouted.

Everyone in the van froze. Charlie stole a glance at his sister. The wrath of a six-year-old was as dangerous and unpredictable as a rabid raccoon. It could not be underestimated. The only way out was a calm demeanor and no sudden movements.

Olive counted to five on her fingers and said, "Now we go."

Ignatius Wisner hustled them over to the boat. A rickety metal gangplank at the stern spanned the pier and the deck on a twenty-degree angle. The captain sent them over it one by one, as if it could not hold up more than a person at a time.

A small and seedy man dragged their bags on board. His name was Cankelton, and he wore a patched-up suit jacket that was two sizes too big. He had a furtive expression, like he expected to be arrested at any moment. Olive refused to let him touch Hello Kitty, lecturing him about the important items that were tightly packed into the kitty's insides. Cankelton avoided her eye while she inventoried down to the last Shopkin.

The deck of the boat looked as if it had been varnished long ago. There were shiny brown strips where the varnish still clung desperately to the wood, and dull gray strips where it had given up and thrown itself overboard. Deck chairs were lined in a row, their faded blue-and-white-striped seats sagging.

A few families stood in a circle, staring down at the deck. The crowd parted, and Charlie saw that somebody's dad had just gone through the canvas of one of the deck chairs. His wife was gamely trying to pull him out of it.

Like a submarine going full-speed ahead, Olive pushed through the crowd and attached herself to the side of a young boy.

"Hi," he said. "I'm Jimmy Jenkins and I'm seven and I like miniature racing cars."

Olive clutched his hand and said, "We'll get married and you can be Jimmy Pennypacker. And stop liking cars. Shopkins are better."

Upon discovering that his name was about to change, his

beloved cars were deep-sixed, and he very suddenly had a fiancée, Jimmy's lip trembled. "I don't want to get married."

"I'm in charge forever and I say we are!"

Olive stomped on Jimmy's foot to make sure he understood that she was in charge forever. He limped back to his mom, engaged and crying.

Mrs. Pennypacker dragged Olive away from her quest to tie Jimmy Jenkins into the knots of holy matrimony. Cankelton showed them to a tight, circular metal staircase that led down to a passageway. The corridor was so narrow that they had to go single file. Flimsy wood doors were named after Disney-like characters such as Don Ducky, Pinnie the Wooh, and Elsie and Annie. The walls were covered in drawings that vaguely resembled Disney characters. Sleeping Beauty looked more dead than asleep while Maleficent leaned over her. Based on Maleficent's tongue sticking out, Charlie made an educated guess that it was a picture of Miley Cyrus cut out of a *People* magazine.

"Here you go," Cankelton said, his eyes shifting everywhere like he had no control over what they did. He handed Mr. Pennypacker and Charlie their sets of keys. "Adjoining cabins. You and your wife are in the Dalmatian Dog suite, and there's a roll-out bed for your daughter, just like you asked."

Charlie wondered if his dad saw the irony of being booked into the Dalmatian Dog suite. The door was painted to look like a dog house, which Mr. Pennypacker was totally in.

"Your son will be next door in Snowed White," Cankelton said. "The other young man will be just across the passageway in Peter Pen and the Lost Boys."

"Exactly where Gunter Hwang belongs," Charlie said. "Lost."

Charlie wasn't thrilled about getting put in Snowed White. He would have preferred some kind of hero, but at least he was getting his own room. Somebody was going to have to watch Olive every minute of the day to make sure she didn't accidently go over the rails. He had worried that she might get pawned off on him.

"I like the Dalmatians," Olive said. "One hundred and one, exactly. Not five like Mrs. Doodles the poodle had last year, but a hundred and one exactly. Everybody can have a puppy! No, wait. I need them all. People can go get their own puppies."

Charlie turned the key in the lock, eager to see his own private cabin.

The first thing that struck him was the larger-than-life lady covering one wall. The painting, titled "Snowed White," depicted a pale person in a white dress sitting on a pile of snow, all outlined in black ink. She was surrounded by her Disney-like dwarves—Distraught, Worried, Agitated, Troubled, Disturbed, Perplexed, Anxious, and Unnerved. They clutched at the bottom of Snowed White's gown like they might pull her down into a demon underworld. Charlie would have to make sure not to look at them too closely when he went to bed or he might become anxious and unnerved himself.

The cabin was small, no bigger than the Pennypackers' upstairs bathroom. There was a twin bed against the bulkhead with built-in drawers underneath. A narrow closet that might hold five hangers was at the foot of the bed and held one book—*A Bloody History of Caribbean Pirates*. A bifold door led to a tiny room with a toilet and sink. Charlie stood in the middle of what little floor space there was. It was not a luxury stateroom, but he could live with it. Especially since he had his own porthole. He would be able to watch the sea from his cabin.

Charlie's spirits began to rise. So what if it wasn't a real Disney cruise? He hadn't cared about seeing Mickey Mouse anyway. He would miss the pool on deck and the AquaDuck, but Wisney Cruises might have some kind of buffet with shrimp, and at least he was going somewhere. He was out of the backyard and going out to sea. He would disembark at foreign ports. He was roaming around the world, and that had to be amazing.

"ONE Dalmatian!" Olive shrieked from the cabin next door. "Where are the rest of them?"

Charlie glanced at the flimsy wall that separated them. He knew from experience that a long negotiation as complicated as a United Nations conference was about to begin regarding the missing Dalmatians. Having witnessed too many of these ill-fated summits, he left his cabin and headed up the stairs.

The deck was deserted. All the other passengers were down below, unpacking. Charlie looked out to sea and imagined what it would be like when they headed out there. The moment they left the dock, they would be attached to nothing and be nowhere. On land, a person was always somewhere. If they were asked, they could look around them and say they were standing in front of the library, or they were in the Maine woods, otherwise known as the Pennypackers' backyard. But out on the ocean there would be no landmarks. The boat would be an infinitesimal speck bobbing around in a watery universe. It was probably how astronauts felt when they were somewhere between the earth and the moon.

Charlie turned back to the pier. In the distance, the captain's black van rumbled toward the boat. It had been driving normally but it began to pick up speed. Charlie supposed Captain Wisner was eager to get back out to sea. The old salt probably didn't feel at home anywhere else.

The van kept going faster and faster, as if the captain had his foot floored on the gas. His driving was beginning to look unhinged.

The van swerved and then straightened out. Charlie squinted and saw two men in dark suits, both carrying briefcases, running behind the van. They didn't seem dressed for a cruise. And if they were going, why didn't Captain Wisner slow down and pick them up?

The van barreled down the dock. The tied-on bumper came loose on one end and bounced along behind. The men shouted something. Charlie couldn't make it out, but it didn't sound friendly.

Charlie gripped the rail. Something was going on. Something bad.

He turned and saw Mr. Pennypacker climbing the stairs

to the deck. Whatever was happening, Charlie did not want his dad to know about it. Mr. Pennypacker took every opportunity to ask for discounts and refunds and tended to escalate the negotiations until there was no turning back. He could just imagine his dad demanding a discount for irregular driving and then making his family get off the boat as a last-ditch bargaining ploy. It would be like the time they were supposed to take the Amtrak train to Boston for his great aunt Myrtle's birthday. Mr. Pennypacker had insisted that Olive should ride free, the conductor insisted that she shouldn't. The Pennypackers had stepped off the train to indicate their steely resolve on the matter. Then they watched the train and their suitcases leave for Boston. The conductor had waved at them as he sailed by.

"Hey, Dad," Charlie said, running across the deck and standing in front of him, blocking his view. "Did you get a television in your cabin?"

Charlie hoped the answer was yes, and then he could suggest that there was a special episode of *Extreme Couponing* coming on. Mr. Pennypacker's primary hobby was maintaining his big folder of coupons, figuring how to double and triple the coupons, and occasionally getting into a flame war on Twitter with his nemesis, @guerrillatacticscouponing.

At the mention of television, a pained look settled over Mr. Pennypacker's features. "No," he said quietly. "Though that reminds me that I'm paying for cable at the house *as we speak* and nobody is even watching it! I wonder if your mom would agree to give it up? Maybe I should just turn it off and see what she says."

Mr. Pennypacker often went on mental wanderings about various opportunities for removing modern life that came with a bill. Charlie was a little surprised that they hadn't ended up dressed in squirrel skins and drawing cave paintings on the side of the house instead of watching cable television.

"Charles," Mrs. Pennypacker called from below, "I could use some help down here explaining about the missing Dalmatians. As Olive keeps pointing out, one hundred of them are lost."

Mr. Pennypacker sighed and turned to go below deck.

Charlie ran back to the railing. The van had pulled far ahead of the running men in dark suits. They began to slow as if they were losing their breath, though they kept pressing on.

Captain Wisner slammed on the brakes, and the van skidded to a stop in front of the boat. He leapt out of the driver's side door and threw open the passenger doors. "Hurry now, Gunter, my boy. The sea waits for nobody."

Chapter Three

Gunter Hwang, next-door-neighbor-ex-friend-backyard-vacation-squealer, was hustled out of the van. Cankelton scurried down the gangplank and grabbed Gunter's backpack.

"Wisner!" one of the men in suits shouted in the distance.

The captain shook his fist at the man and pushed Gunter onto the gangplank.

Cankelton threw the backpack over the railing, and Charlie heard the quiet tinkling of breaking glass. He crossed his fingers that it was Gunter's phone.

Captain Wisner lumbered over the gangplank, his weight causing it to sag. As soon as he hit the deck, Cankelton followed him, reeled in the gangplank, and raced to the stern.

The captain jogged to the bow. They threw off the lines, and the current carried the boat a few feet from the dock.

The men in suits were huffing and puffing their way down the long pier. One of them had even thrown his briefcase away in a bid to go faster. Captain Wisner climbed up to the bridge and frantically worked the controls. The engines roared to life as the men reached the end of the dock.

Both men stared at the growing distance between the boat and the dock as if they were analyzing their chances of being able to leap on. The shorter man shook his head.

"Captain Ignatius Wisner," the taller one called. "You can't avoid us forever. *Nobody* avoids us forever. We'll catch up to you eventually!"

The boat drifted ever farther from the dock. Captain Wisner leaned out a window and called, "Not today, wise guy!"

The taller man kicked at the dock. Charlie got the feeling this was not the first time they had chased after Captain Wisner. But why? Who were they and what did they want?

Whatever the captain was involved in, under no circumstances could Charlie allow Mr. Pennypacker to find out about it. They would be off the boat in seconds, and Mr. Pennypacker would demand a full refund and then press his wife to file a lawsuit. As he had told Charlie more than once, "Let some company wrong me or make me sick or sell me a lemon-car and I will sue and we will be set for life." Mr. Pennypacker's dream was to suffer reversible kidney damage so he could win a large settlement and then afterward get his kidneys back in shape like nothing ever happened.

The men turned and walked dejectedly back down the pier. The one who had thrown down his briefcase picked it up and shook it at the boat. Captain Wisner brandished his fist out the window by way of an answer and swung the boat around toward open sea.

Charlie and Gunter were the only passengers who had seen what happened.

Now Gunter turned and stared at Charlie.

"What are *you* doing here?" Charlie asked, even though he knew perfectly well what Gunter was doing there.

"You're one to talk," Gunter said. "What are *you* doing here? You're supposed to be spray-painting your backyard white and pretending you went to the Swiss Alps."

Charlie did not respond to that accusation as it hit a little too close to home. His dad had suggested something similar, only they were going to pretend they were in the Poconos. They would grease the bottom of their toboggan with Crisco and push each other down the small slope in the backyard.

"Oh, wait a minute," Gunter said. "I forgot about the note on the mailbox. You're supposed to be cruising in a luxury stateroom." Gunter snorted. "Like I would have ever bought that one."

Charlie cringed as he thought of his note. Until he remembered that Gunter was on the same boat as Charlie.

"News flash," Charlie said, "your dad is just as cheap as mine, otherwise you wouldn't be on this Disney-like 'Wisney' cruise, either."

"It's not Disney-like or Wisney-like, it's a Wisner cruise, as in the captain's last name," Gunter said. "Me and my dad come every year."

"You should have checked the side of the boat. It says *Wisney Cruise*, as in *Disney* with a *W*."

"What's Disney got to do with it?" Gunter asked.

"Disney has everything to do with it."

"No, it doesn't," Gunter said. "This is a fishing boat."

"Well, today," Charlie said, "this is an almost-like-Disney cruise."

"That's ridiculous," Gunter said. "As usual, Pennypacker, you have totally lost the plot."

Behind him, Charlie heard his mom say, "Slow down, hon, I can't keep up with you."

Olive said, "Mickey! There you are. Where is Minnie? I want to talk to her."

Charlie turned to see a tall, redheaded man dressed in red jeans, a black tuxedo jacket, and white gloves. He wore the kind of mouse ears that kids bought at Disneyland.

"I dunno, kid," the man said to Olive. "Minnie's probably at the House of Pancakes spending the last of my money. That's where she usually is. Why pancakes? They're filling, I guess."

"Wait a minute," Olive said, stamping her foot. "The real Mickey Mouse has big black feet and he has a whole different face! He has a mouse face, not a people face. You're not Mickey Mouse."

The man leaned against the railing and said, "I'm Mickey Mouse-*r*. With an *r*. Get the difference?"

Charlie turned back to Gunter and folded his arms.

Gunter stared at the redheaded Mickey Mouser and whispered, "Who is that guy? Where's Brad? What the heck is going on?"

"What is going on," Charlie said, "is that my dad booked

us on this cheap knockoff Disney-like cruise and your family did the same thing. What I'd like to know is how come you've been making fun of *my* vacations when you come on this stupid thing every year? Also, am I really supposed to believe that you've been to Germany and South Korea? You probably just come here and buy T-shirts off the internet, *Mr. Worldwide*."

Gunter ignored Charlie's accusation. He was staring at Mickey Mouser with an *r*. "It's supposed to be just a bunch of guys. We lounge around and fish and everybody's dirty and sweaty and Brad cooks whatever we catch."

"Right," Charlie said. "Just Brad and a bunch of dirty, sweaty guys on a boat called *Aladdin's Dream*?"

"That's not the name of it," Gunter said. "It's the *Kingfisher*."

"Not anymore," Charlie said.

Gunter stared at Charlie. Then he hung over the railing to get a look. *"Aladdin's Dream?"*

Charlie briefly wondered if he could heave him overboard without getting in trouble.

Gunter put his feet back on deck and turned to Charlie. "Something has gone really wrong. First those two suits chase after the van, now the boat's name is changed, the crew is new, and they're dressed in weird costumes. I have to figure out what's going on."

"Do whatever," Charlie said.

"You're so transparent," Gunter said. "Obviously, you're trying to make me think you're not trying to figure it out. Well, I have *my* own ideas already."

"I'm not trying anything," Charlie said.

"Right," Gunter said.

"I guess we'll see," Charlie said.

"We *will* see," Gunter said.

"I'm sure we will."

"I know I will see. It is a fact that I will see."

Charlie knew that once "we will see" came into a conversation with Gunter, it could go on forever in an endless loop of what Gunter would see. If there were a "have the last word" Olympics, Gunter Hwang would come home with the gold every time.

Charlie turned and walked away. He got to the opposite side of the boat and watched the port get farther and farther from view. Passengers began to come up from below, and Captain Wisner came on the loudspeaker.

"Folks," he said, "welcome aboard *Aladdin's Dream*. We

have such an amazing trip planned that people literally chased me down the pier to try to get on our boat. Which, if you happened to notice it, was absolutely nothing to be alarmed about."

Charlie glanced at Gunter. Gunter saw him looking and then rubbed his chin thoughtfully, like he was already on his way to figuring out what was going on. Charlie rolled his eyes in response.

"Even now, as we speak," the captain continued, "we barrel straight ahead into open ocean, cruising in high style. In a mere two hours, you will hear the chow bell—I mean, the dinner gong, and you will make your way to the mess hall—I mean, our stately dining room. There, you will dine with some of your favorite Disney-like characters. After a restful night in your richly appointed staterooms, you will wake to find yourself in the beautiful Bahamas, where you will be taken on a snorkeling adventure by our own lovely Cinderalla. Go ahead and congratulate yourselves for selecting Wisney Cruises."

His dad made his way over to Charlie. "Did you hear that?" Mr. Pennypacker said. "We'll wake up in the Bahamas. We are rolling like royalty."

Charlie snorted. "Royalty? What does *your* cabin look like? I already know that it's missing a hundred Dalmatians."

"All right," his dad admitted. "Royalty is a stretch. But after all, are we really royalty kind of people?"

"Not on your watch, we aren't," Charlie said.

"I'll have you know," Mr. Pennypacker said, "that thanks to Gunter's dad, I booked this trip on AbsolutelyWayCheap estCheapestCaribbeanVacationsCheapestImACheapskate .com. A very reputable site known for unbeatable value. You heard it from the captain himself—people were literally chasing him to go on this trip, and so you're welcome, son."

Charlie didn't want his dad to think too hard about people chasing the captain, which might lead to ideas about a lawsuit. To turn his attention, he said, "What are you going to do about Olive? She's not buying Mickey Mouser with an *r*."

Mr. Pennypacker's brow furrowed. "Well, she hasn't met Cinderalla yet, so fingers crossed. Ah, there's Gunter. I'd better go give him the list of rules—his dad will fine me five dollars a day if he comes back sick or injured. I lose the whole thing if he doesn't come back at all."

As the boat rumbled out to sea, Charlie breathed in the salt air and felt the warm breeze on his face. They were on their way. They were on a real vacation, heading off into the unknown. There was no AquaDuck, but he could watch the sea for dolphins and whales and be the first to spot exotic ports on the horizon. He might even see plankton phosphorescence or the mysterious green flash at sunset some people claimed they'd seen.

Everything was falling into place. The men in suits were left behind, it was too late for his dad to change his mind and take them off the boat, and Gunter wouldn't bother him much. Gunter would spend the whole trip trying to solve the mystery of the men in suits because he'd said he would. Once Gunter had thrown down a challenge, he'd doggedly pursue it even if it was totally stupid. And it was usually totally stupid.

It would be like the time two people had cruised down their street, emptying the neighborhood recycle bins into the trunk of their car. Gunter had staked out his front yard for a week. When they came back again, he'd dramatically thrown himself on the hood of their Toyota Corolla and dialed 911, only to find out it was people from the next block who needed the old newspapers for a litter of puppies they were cleaning up after.

· · ·

The stately dining room was a narrow rectangle with a single row of picnic tables running the length and bolted to the floor. There were more Disney-like drawings along the walls, including one in which the artist had appeared to run out of interest. As best Charlie could figure, it was the beginnings of a portrait of Goofy. At the moment, it consisted of only two large, square teeth.

The far end of the dining hall led to an open galley, and it appeared that red-haired Mickey Mouser was also the chef. So far, that did not look promising. His mouse ears hung around his neck as he threw four packs of hotdogs into boiling water. He stared into the water for a few seconds, then pulled the hot dogs out again and took them out of their plastic wrappers.

Worse than that, though, were the seating arrangements. All the kids, and the sort-of-like-Disney characters, were forced to sit together. Parents were seated at the opposite end of the tables.

Charlie was next to Olive and across from Gunter, which was as far away as he could get. On his other side were two sullen twins of about eight. They had already announced that their names were Patience and Prudence and they didn't like anybody except each other and they had their own language called Cucuchara, which they would not teach Charlie, no matter how much he begged. Charlie had pointed out that no one was begging, but they just turned toward each other and screeched.

An older girl named Claire sat next to Gunter. She looked to her other side at the apparition sitting next to her and said, "Hashtag: what the what?" It appeared to be Cankelton, dressed as the surprising offspring of a cockroach and a wasp. He had large wings that prevented him from leaning back in his chair and two long feelers that kept falling in front of his face. Six legs were sewn down the front of his costume. They waved in all directions every time he moved, like they didn't know which way they wanted to go.

Jimmy Jenkins was hiding on the other side of the twins to avoid having to marry Olive. Olive had not yet noticed her fiancé, as she was listing all the Disney characters who wanted to be her best friend.

She counted off on her fingers, "Elsa, Anna, Ariel, Belle, Princess Jasmine, Cinderella, Merida, and Tiana. And I'm going to tell Merida that we need to trade hair."

Olive looked around the table for any of these new best friends, but only found Cankelton. She frowned. "Why are you scary?" she asked him.

Cankelton moved the feelers out of his eyes and said, "Not scary, miss. Just pathetic."

"What are you?" Olive asked.

"A cricket," Cankelton said softly.

Gunter snorted. "Cankelton, are you really supposed to be Jiminy Cricket? For real?"

"*Timiny* Cricket," Cankelton said, shifting his eyes around the cabin.

"But why?" Gunter asked. "What's going on? What happened to fishing? Where's Brad and Clarissa? Why has everything changed?"

"Timiny Cricket knows nothing!" Cankelton said in a high, squeaky voice that sounded like he might be turning into an actual cricket.

Olive, apparently bored with the conversation, started twisting her hair around her fingers to try to make it curl like Merida's. Charlie was relieved that her attention was focused on her hair and she had not yet noticed Cinderalla, who was smoking a cigarette near a porthole.

Charlie had hoped, for all of their sakes, that Cinderalla might have some passing resemblance to the real Cinderella. In the best-case scenario, she'd be a tall blonde in an elaborate ball gown wearing the usual glass slippers. She was blond, but

that was where the resem-
blance ended. Cinderalla,
if that was her real name,
was darkly tanned, and
her complexion had a leath-
ery appearance. Her bleached
hair looked crispy, like it had been
deep-fried, and Charlie wondered if
it would bend or just crumble into
dust. Her dress was shiny pale
blue and looked like a cheap
Halloween costume from the
drugstore—the type that hangs
limp and looks more like a
nightgown. The pack of Marlboros peeking out of one of the
pockets did nothing to help
what was already a pretty
alarming picture. There were no glass slippers in sight;
Cinderalla wore black flip-flops and had painted her toe-
nails black to match.

Charlie watched her take one last drag of her cigarette,
smash it into an ashtray, and slap a plastic tiara on her head.

"Hey, kids," she said in a throaty voice, throwing herself onto the bench across from Olive. "Cinderalla here."

"Wait, what?" Claire said. She dug her phone from her purse and snapped a picture. "Hashtag: Cinderella got old."

Olive narrowed her eyes at Cinderalla. Mr. Pennypacker watched nervously from the other end of the dining hall.

In a voice cold enough to chill a villain's heart, Olive said, "WHERE IS THE PRINCE?"

Chapter Four

Olive leaned forward, her eyes boring into Cinderalla's face.

"Uh . . . where's the prince?" Cinderalla said, clearly not expecting this curveball.

"The prince," Olive said grimly.

Cinderalla looked anxiously around the table, as if somebody else would tell Olive the prince's exact whereabouts. Everybody remained silent, awed by Olive's deadly stare.

Cinderalla finally shrugged and said, "Cripes, how should I know? I've been waiting for my prince to come along for years, but it's just been one frog after another."

Charlie braced himself for the explosion. He guessed that Olive would surpass the meltdown she'd had when she got the wrong American Girl doll for her birthday. She had pinned her hopes on songbird Melody, and the Pennypackers found out the hard way that imaginative Maryellen didn't measure up. After tears, and then a long lecture on the superiority of Melody, poor Maryellen had been forced to stay in her box and live in darkness under Olive's bed. In the end, Mr. Pennypacker ended up more traumatized than Olive, as this was yet another purchase made by Mrs. Pennypacker via a bidding war on eBay.

Charlie gave his dad the thumbs-down so he would be prepared for the evening storms that were about to roll in.

Olive suddenly slapped her forehead and cried, "You don't know yet! That's why you're dressed in rags! You're still a servant living in the attic with the mice!"

"What?" Cinderalla asked.

"That's why you have on that ugly dress," Olive said, "you've been cleaning for your evil stepmother! Don't worry, your fairy godmother is gonna fix up your face and get you a pretty dress and glass slippers so the prince will fall in love with you."

"Fix my face?" Cinderalla said, reaching up to touch one of her weather-worn cheeks.

"Yeah," Olive said. "But it's not your fault! You've been working day and night."

Cinderalla took in a long, slow breath. "Tell me about it. I'm exhausted. How am I supposed to entertain kids, keep all those cabins clean by myself, and on top of that, learn how to snorkel while leading an excursion? Did I put 'good swimmer' on my résumé? No, I did not."

Olive studied Cinderalla. Then she said, "In the movie, you don't look so bad when you're doin' all the cleaning. What happened?"

"Life happened," Cinderalla said darkly.

Charlie began to fear that they had more to worry about than Olive falling overboard. Cinderalla might *throw* her overboard.

"Well," Olive said, turning her attention to her hot dog and potato chips, "at least you got a fairy godmother. It's gonna be happily ever after for you!"

"Is it?" Cinderalla asked. "I used to believe that. Now I'm not so sure."

Olive didn't reply. Instead, she focused on drawing a line of ketchup across her hot dog. Her interest in another person's existential crisis was reliably zero.

The twins began a rapid-fire conversation in Cucuchara. Claire attempted to take a photo of them, but she decided against it after they screeched at her like wild animals and tried to rip her phone from her hands.

Gunter leaned over to Cinderalla and said, "Why were those two guys in suits chasing after the captain?"

Charlie hid a smile. Just as he had predicted, Gunter would spend his entire vacation on a pointless quest, convinced that Charlie was doing the same thing and determined to beat him at it.

When he and Gunter had been friends, there had been way too many competitions. His own mom and dad couldn't care less whether Charlie won or lost a soccer match. Mr. Pennypacker only wanted to know if they were on the hook for snacks and how much was *that* going to cost.

The Hwangs, on the other hand, took a dim view of losing. Nothing that could be won should ever be lost. Charlie had not cared whether he won or lost an Edge of the World tournament or a breath-holding challenge or a race to the nearest telephone pole. Though he *had* been bothered that the Hwangs always looked sorry for him, like he was the pathetic loser next door.

Gunter folded his arms. "Well? Why is the captain getting chased?"

Cinderalla shrugged. She either didn't know or wasn't going to say why the men had chased the van.

Gunter turned to Charlie. "Listening in on my interrogation? Getting me to do all the heavy lifting, as usual, Pennypacker?"

"I actually don't care," Charlie said.

"Right."

"Really. I don't."

"We will see," Gunter said.

"I guess so," Charlie said.

Olive raised her hot dog in the air and shouted, "Stop talking! You're ruining the Disney mood!"

Cinderalla rolled her eyes and went to smoke another cigarette.

"Game on," Gunter whispered.

. . .

The next morning, Charlie opened his eyes. He had slept with the porthole cracked open and now he felt a warm, salty breeze drift in. He jumped on his knees and looked out.

He was surrounded by pale blue water. Two hundred

yards ahead, a white beach ran in either direction, backed by a jungle of palm trees. There was nobody on the beach and no houses he could see. It was like the kind of tropical paradises he'd seen on TV. His only other experience with a beach was the one time he went on a day trip to Seaside Heights with his friend Kyle's family. That beach had been a sea of umbrellas. Old men were stretched out on beach chairs doing a slow broil to well-done, mothers chased children determined to drown themselves, and two lifeguards spent the day wildly blowing their whistles. The carnival music from the rides along the boardwalk and the smells of Italian sausage and caramel corn had hung in the air.

Here, the beach was empty and silent, and the air only smelled of sea salt. It wouldn't have surprised him to see the cast of *Survivor* walk out of the trees and start building a camp with their bare hands.

Charlie stuck his head out the porthole and peered down into the water below to the white, sandy bottom. Oval-shaped blue fish schooled around the hull, as if they were grateful to find some unexpected shade. Small waves made a cheerful slip-slap against the hull.

Charlie smiled. He had made it. He was at a foreign destination. It was a magical morning in the tropics.

"Where are they?" Olive shouted from the adjoining cabin.

"Where are the hundred lost Dalmatians? You said they would come back in the night!"

"I said maybe they would," Mr. Pennypacker answered. "Dogs are notoriously unreliable."

Charlie sighed. He supposed Olive could drain the magic out of any morning.

He jumped out of bed and opened the menu that had been left in his room. It said they were going to have a "Continental Breakfast." He assumed *continental* meant Europe, hopefully France. The French were the world's bravest food adventurers. He'd seen a show where a guy had actually eaten a fried cow pancreas. Charlie didn't know if he would be served a pancreas or a cow's tongue or tripe or goose liver. Whatever it was, even if it looked disgusting, he was going to try it.

As it turned out, the continental breakfast was a slapped together egg sandwich and an apple. Chef Mickey Mouser staggered around the galley pulling toast from the toaster, bumping into counters and cracking eggs that sometimes ended up in a pan and sometimes didn't. Cinderalla sat at the table sullenly drinking black coffee. She had a mug in front of her and another one lined up behind it, ready to go.

Claire lifted the top piece of toast off her limp sandwich and snapped a photo. "Hashtag: sad sandwich."

The twins stared at their apples, shrieked at each other, and then threw them over their shoulders. Jimmy Jenkins ran after them like a dog chasing a ball.

Gunter leaned over to Cinderalla and whispered, "Why were those guys in suits chasing the van yesterday?"

Cinderalla shrugged. "How should I know?" she said, her voice raspy. "He probably owes taxes. Every year I don't file and every year I think this is the year they'll catch up to me. But hey, that's what's good about being a yachtie—you're elusive."

"The IRS," Gunter said. "I should have known that was it."

Charlie knew for a fact it wasn't the IRS. His dad was an accountant and he liked to "sail close to the wind" on his taxes. He had told Charlie more than once that if he saw an envelope from the Internal Revenue Service, the jig was up. The IRS, he said, sent all bad news by mail.

"Why is there a new crew? What happened to Clarissa?" Gunter asked. "She used to clean the cabins and leave a snack-sized bag of M&M's on my pillow every day."

"She sounds like she goes the extra mile," Cinderalla said. "Ratchet down your hopes—I don't go any mile."

"But where is she? And where is Brad? He used to be the cook, not that red-haired guy."

Cinderalla looked down at her ballgown/nightgown. "Maybe they got sick of the costumes."

"There weren't any costumes before," Gunter said.

"I dunno, kid," Cinderalla said. "All I know is I'm supposed to take the guests snorkeling and I gotta go read about how the equipment works. And try to remember how swimming works. I ain't what you'd call a natural in the water—a bathtub is the deep end as far as I'm concerned."

Cinderalla downed her second cup of coffee, which Charlie assumed was enough rocket fuel to fuel an actual rocket, and then dragged herself out of the room.

"I saw you listening," Gunter said, staring at Charlie.

"I have ears, don't I?" Charlie said. "Not that you found out anything."

"I did too find out. Those guys were from the IRS."

"Wrong," Charlie said.

"You don't know it's wrong," Gunter said. "Wherever those guys are from, I will find out," Gunter said.

"Uh-huh," Charlie said.

"We'll see," Gunter said.

"We'll see what?" Charlie asked, stymied again by how his conversations with Gunter ended with a "we will see" every single time.

"You better believe we'll see," Gunter said.

"We won't see anything. I'm not interested."

"Still sticking to that story, are you?" Gunter said, folding his arms. "Let's just find out how not interested you really are when I get to tell everybody what's been going on. Your poor dad will have to realize, again, that his son is a loser who can't figure anything out."

Charlie's head snapped up. What did his dad have to do with it? Why would Gunter need to tell his dad anything? He'd known Gunter would be like a dog with a bone about those men. He hadn't anticipated Gunter wanting to tell his

dad about whatever he found out. Mr. Pennypacker would jump on any kind of information Gunter came up with and start dreaming up lawsuits. Hadn't his dad thought there might be a case against the people who took newspapers out of his recycle bin? He'd claimed a litter of puppies was no legal defense and only gave it up when Charlie's mom pointed out exactly how low a judgment for old newspapers would be. Mr. Pennypacker would have the whole family off the boat and headed to court at the next port. The vacation would be over.

He had to put a stop to Gunter's investigation. He had to figure out who those men were before Gunter did. If there was one thing Charlie knew about Gunter Hwang, it was that if Charlie beat him to the answer, Gunter wouldn't want anybody to know he lost the competition, including Mr. Pennypacker.

But Gunter had a real advantage. He'd been on the boat a bunch of times before. He might have some guesses already. Charlie would have to move fast to get ahead of him.

He paused. What was his first move? He'd go ask the captain. It might be as simple as that. Captain Wisner might be able to put this whole stupid mystery to bed in five minutes with Mr. Pennypacker none the wiser.

Charlie got up and walked toward the door, leaving Gunter

behind. He passed Olive, who was lecturing Mickey Mouser because the egg in her sandwich was runny and that was the same as eating a raw baby bird and Olive Pennypacker did not eat baby birds because she loved all the babies in the world.

Mickey Mouser stuck his hand out and muttered, "Give me your plate, you little dictator."

Charlie ran down the long corridor and up the winding stairs to the deck. The boat rocked gently on the sea, the sun warmed the top of his head, and, standing there alone with the sea to his back and the shoreline ahead, he could almost imagine he was a pirate considering where to bury his treasure. There was no way he would let Gunter ruin this trip.

Chapter Five

Charlie made his way to the metal staircase that led up to the bridge and jogged to the top. Ignatius Wisner sat in his captain's chair with his feet up, balancing a cup of coffee on his belly.

Charlie cleared his throat.

The captain slid down on his chair, just catching his cup of coffee before it tipped over. He sat up and swung around to Charlie.

"Ah-ha!" he cried. "I spy a young man who could not keep himself away from the bridge. I suppose you have dreams of captaining your own vessel someday? Most natural thing in the world."

"Uh, no," Charlie said. "I just wanted to ask you a question."

"Of course you do," the captain said in a hearty voice. "What boy doesn't have questions? Why, a young man your age is practically a question factory. Now, do I know what those questions are? You bet, son. One, how deep is the water below the boat? Two, how far are we from Miami? Three, are there sharks and, if so, are they dangerous? Four, is a knot how far or how fast? And, of course, five, how much will you get paid if you join the Coast Guard?"

The Coast Guard? It had never occurred to Charlie to join the Coast Guard. "No, Captain, I just wanted to know—"

"Thirty-six feet deep, 186 miles from Miami, sharks all over the place—tiger sharks, hammerheads, blacktip reef sharks, bull sharks, and lemon sharks. Yes, they're dangerous—they *are* sharks after all. But rest assured, my good fellow, your chances of being attacked by a shark are one in eleven and a half million."

The captain laid his finger along the side of his nose as if he were about to tell Charlie a secret. "Naturally," he said, "that statistic about shark attacks is rather cold comfort for the unlucky one in that eleven and a half million."

Charlie supposed that was true. If you were attacked by a shark, it really wouldn't help to know how slim the chances had been.

"Now," the captain continued, "a knot is all about speed. It's equal to one nautical mile, which is about one point one five miles per hour. Why not just use miles per hour? Who knows; probably because it would be too easy. Thinking about joining the Coast Guard, are you? Many young men do. Sadly, it's not a get-rich-quick scheme. You'll make about twenty thousand your first year, which seems low, considering you'll be risking your life. But what can you do when you're called to adventure? You've got to answer the call!"

Charlie was overwhelmed by the information erupting from the captain like a volcano. "No," he stuttered. "I mean, that's all interesting, but not what I wanted to ask. What I wanted to know was—"

"Whoa, look at the time!" Captain Wisner exclaimed, pointing at his watch. "Nine twenty-two and a half already. My morning announcement is scheduled for twenty-two and a half minutes after nine on the dot. Marine living is all about schedules, my boy. Throw away the schedule and what have you got? A schedule-less vessel, which is no good to anybody. Now hustle yourself down to your cabin, jump into some swimming trunks, and prepare yourself for an unparalleled underwater safari."

Charlie staggered down the stairs. He hardly knew how

the captain had managed to get him off the bridge before he could ask a single question about the men in suits.

The captain's voice boomed over the loudspeaker. "Good morning, good morning, good morning, folks! I hope you have enjoyed our spectacular continental breakfast prepared by our own Chef Mickey and are ready for a day filled with incredible sights and sounds. You find yourself this beautiful morning on a remote beach in the Bahamas. Can your larger cruise ships take you to such a paradise? No, folks. No, they cannot. The water's too shallow for those oversized contraptions. But here *we* are! If you will meet Cinderalla on the aft deck at precisely ten o'clock, she will lead you to the dinghy and you will be on your way to discovering the attractions of our undersea world. This is not to be missed, people! Bahamian fish are world famous for being interesting. As always, safety first—if you're afraid of the water, have a tendency to drown, or have had any near-drowning experiences in the past, including falling through lake ice or falling in your shower, inform Cinderalla so that she and Mickey Mouser can be prepared to execute any emergency measures that might be required."

Charlie stood on the deck listening to the captain's speech. How was Cinderalla supposed to save anybody when she was trying to remember how to swim and was just now reading a book on how to snorkel?

"Beauty and adventure and magical Disney-like characters," the captain continued. "That's what Wisney Cruises is all about. Over and out."

. . .

A half hour later, Charlie was back on deck in his swim trunks. Olive had just been informed that she was not old enough to snorkel and did not have the water skills to attempt it.

"If I'm not going, nobody is going!" she shrieked.

Everyone froze. Satisfied that she had everybody's attention, Olive dramatically wailed at the sky, clutched her hair in her fists, and then delivered the finale by lying on the deck while holding her breath. It was a first-class performance and plans were hastily made for Mrs. Pennypacker to take Olive to the beach to play in the shallow water.

Charlie's dad said he was going to stay on board and use the opportunity to take the nap he had been trying to take for the past ten years. Charlie didn't buy it, though. His dad was not a napper. He assumed what Mr. Pennypacker would really be doing was calculating his losses. Paying for cable nobody was watching = lost money. Paying for car insurance when nobody was driving = lost money. Charlie assumed that by the time they got back from snorkeling, there would be a whole lecture prepared about how much food was going bad in their refrigerator.

Getting everybody to shore had taken two trips on the rubber dinghy, with Mickey Mouser quietly cursing at the tiller and Cinderalla sitting at the bow smoking. She did not seem to care that once the dinghy started moving, the wind blew the smoke from bow to stern and so really, everybody was smoking.

After they had all made it to the beach, Charlie wrestled himself into his swim fins and staggered toward the water. He fell on the sand twice before he got the hang of lifting his feet high enough to avoid tripping. Then he watched Gunter walk into the water and put his fins on once he was waist deep.

"I know I could've done it that way," Charlie said. "But it exercises my muscles to do it my way."

"What muscles?" Gunter asked.

Cinderalla stood in the water and held up a mask. "This here," she said, "you put on your face. And this thing," she said, pointing at the snorkel, "is what you breathe from. Put it in your mouth. Now, once you're swimmin' around, you're gonna see fish. Tropical type of fish. The kind of fish that . . . live around here. Great! Nobody has any questions so go ahead and get snorkeling."

"She doesn't know what she's doing," Gunter said quietly. "You have to spit in the mask and rub it around or else it will fog up. She didn't even say how to clear water from a snorkel after you dive down."

Charlie snorted. "Spit in my mask? I'm not that gullible," he said.

Gunter shrugged and swam away. Charlie put his mask on his face and his snorkel in his mouth and pushed off the sand, lying facedown in the water. At first, he didn't see anything except the crisscross pattern of light dancing on the bottom. He slowly drifted over a rocky formation and saw some small blue and orange fish hanging around it. The fish began to fade into a gray cloud as his mask fogged up. He stood up and took it off.

Looking around, all he saw were people floating facedown like they had all died in a shipwreck. Except for Olive, who was up to her knees in water while his mom watched from a beach chair. His sister appeared to have unpacked some sandwiches from the cooler. She was deconstructing them and throwing bread and meat into the water. It was like she was feeding the ducks, without any ducks.

Gunter was farther out than anybody else, diving down and then coming back up again and blowing water out of his snorkel like he was a breaching whale. And like the show-off he always was.

Charlie made sure Gunter wasn't looking, then spit in his mask, rubbed it around, and rinsed it out. Putting his head back in the water, the fog was gone. Not that he would tell Gunter that.

As Charlie floated on his stomach and stared at the ocean floor, one of the rocks moved. He kept still, watching. It moved again. Charlie brushed away a piece of ham floating past his mask. The shape of what was moving became clear, like one of those pictures where first

you see one image and then you see another and wonder why you didn't see the second one right away. A mottled white-and-brown octopus was tucked into a crevice with just one eye showing and three arms full of suction cups draped around the rocks.

It gave him a baleful stare.

Charlie had the sudden urge to show Gunter. It would be cool to point out something he had found that nobody else had seen. It would be especially cool to show it to Gunter, who thought he was such a snorkeling expert.

Just as he was about to call Gunter, Charlie stopped himself. If he showed the octopus to him, Gunter might think Charlie was trying to be friends like they used to be. Which Charlie would never do. He had a new best friend. His name was Kyle Kendreth and he was an excellent friend. Kyle and his amazing mom were

nothing like the Hwangs. Kyle's mom thought everything Charlie and Kyle did was fantastic. She said it was a toss-up which one of them would end up being president of the United States. One time, Charlie had even come home from a sleepover at Kyle's with a participation trophy. He was named MVP for not breaking anything expensive. Kyle didn't make fun of the Pennypackers' fake vacations. Kyle's mom called Mr. Pennypacker's ideas "highly original."

As Charlie circled his octopus, a scream split the air like an ear-piercing siren. He yanked his head out of the water. Something thrashed in the shallow water in front of Olive. The water roiled and sprayed up into the air like the sea had turned into a washing machine. Olive stood frozen, staring at the maelstrom.

Two tall gray fins with black tips emerged. They looked like . . . shark fins.

Chapter Six

Olive threw the sandwiches left in her hand into the churning water in front of her. Mrs. Pennypacker launched herself out of her chair as if she were aboard a rocket-propelled missile. She yanked Olive out of the sea.

Cinderalla saw the shark fins and began to sink, waving her arms around like she was a drowning seaman flagging down a passing ship. Gunter swam over to her and held her up. Mickey Mouser, who had been sunbathing on shore next to the dinghy, pushed it into the water, jumped in, and started the engine.

Cinderalla gripped Gunter's hair in both hands and screamed, "Get me out of the water!"

Gunter shook her and shouted, "Don't flail around! You're kicking up the sand and clouding up the water. Those sharks will think you're a dying fish and won't be able to see they're wrong. By the time they figure out their mistake you'll be bleeding to death."

Charlie looked around. The sharks had disappeared. Where did they go?

Though he was generally against any opinion of Gunter's, Charlie worried about the sand he was kicking up while trying to walk out of the water in his fins. He carefully slipped them off and let go of them. The swim fins drifted on the surface of the water behind him while Charlie slowly moved toward shore, trying not to seem like a dying fish.

"They're after the meat Olive threw in the water," Gunter shouted.

Charlie looked around him. He was surrounded by cold cuts. Slices of ham, roast beef, turkey, and chunks of tuna salad floated by.

Mrs. Pennypacker, still carrying Olive, had run down the beach and now stood directly in front of Charlie. "Get out, Charlie!" she screamed.

"I'm trying not to kick up the sand, mom," Charlie shouted back. He moved slowly and deliberately to shore while scanning the surface of the water all around him. The sharks were there somewhere, he just couldn't see where.

He heard an explosive splash behind him and turned his head. One of his swim fins had disappeared. Seconds later, it reappeared, a perfect half circle of teeth marks taken out of the blue rubber.

Charlie lost his nerve and flailed and crawled the rest of the way out of the water. Mrs. Pennypacker grabbed him into a viselike grip.

Gunter dragged Cinderalla onto the beach. Two black-tipped shark fins broke the surface twenty yards offshore. Charlie watched his other swim fin disappear and then pop back up, rejected. Blobs of cold cuts vanished in a feeding frenzy. The sharks were following the meat as it slowly drifted out to sea.

Mickey Mouser had accomplished nothing, other than driving the dinghy in circles and nearly running over the twins before beaching it again.

Once everybody was safely out of the water, the twins screeched at each other in Cucuchara. Charlie couldn't understand it, but he thought the gist of it was that they now hated snorkeling, Cinderalla, sharks, Mickey Mouser, and the dinghy.

Cinderalla had to be laid down on a towel. She had Mickey Mouser by the hair and shook him. "What if they come back?"

she asked. "How far up the beach could they get? Should we all climb trees?"

Mickey Mouser unpeeled her fingers from his hair and shouted, "Everybody stand back while I perform CPR!"

Cinderalla slapped his leg. "How could I be talking if my heart stopped beating, you idiot."

Mickey Mouser considered this very valid point and said, "Revised! Everybody stand back while I *don't* perform CPR. Get me the first aid kit—this victim needs oxygen, stat!"

Charlie ran to the dinghy to get the large green box with a red cross on it. It was heavy, and he had to drag it across the sand to Mickey. Mickey threw it open and attached the tubing and mask to the tank and cranked the valve open. He stared at the pressure gauge, then said, "Revised! The tank is empty, so stand back while I apply rescue breathing!"

"Get away from me, you creepster," Cinderalla said. "Go get my cigarettes."

"Somebody go get Cinderalla's cigarettes! Stat!"

Claire flipped her braids over her shoulder and said, "Hashtag: Jaws here."

Then everybody turned to Olive.

Gunter said, "You were chumming the water, you little maniac. You could have gotten us all killed."

"I was feeding the fish because I love them," Olive said, her tone full of the defiance she generally trotted out when she was accused of something she knew she did.

"You were feeding *sharks*," Gunter said.

"Now, hold on," Mrs. Pennypacker said. "You can't blame Olive. She's only six."

"Yeah," Olive said, her face brightening. "I'm only six. I can't be blamed."

All eyes turned to Mrs. Pennypacker, who Charlie had to admit was indeed the responsible party.

"Sorry, mommy," Olive said. "I'm only six so you're gonna get blamed."

"For heaven's sake," Mrs. Pennypacker said. "I was just trying to relax. Yes, I saw her throw a couple of sandwiches into the water, but so what? It didn't seem dangerous. If any of you had a six-year-old, you would know that any activity that grabs their attention, short of setting a fire, climbing on the roof, or attempting to drive the car, can afford a very much-needed break."

Cinderalla was still prone on her towel and was now blowing smoke rings into the air. "Really?" she said between coughs. "Just because she wasn't driving, it seemed like a good idea?"

"Well, maybe, *Cinderalla*," Mrs. Pennypacker said, "you should have put *don't throw sandwiches into the water* into your not very extensive briefing."

Mickey Mouser said, "Listen here everybody, I have executed my safety officer duties to the letter, and there have been no casualties. So congratulations to me and there's no use playing the blame game. The sharks are gone—following a trail of lunch meat out to sea. Hopefully, they have not learned to associate people with delicious cold cuts. Little Olive has learned her lesson and will never again throw lunch into the water or complain about her egg sandwich at breakfast."

"I can complain if I want to," Olive whispered.

Despite Mickey's assurances that the sharks were gone, nobody had the nerve to go back into the water. There might have been the opportunity to have a picnic on the beach, but it turned out that Olive had thrown away more sandwiches than Mrs. Pennypacker had realized. Mickey took the two that were left and cut them into a mouthful for each person.

As Charlie chewed his morsel of ham on white bread, Gunter sidled over and said, "I saw you spit in your mask so it wouldn't fog up, just like I told you," he said.

"I didn't spit in my mask," Charlie answered. He was not sure why he lied about it, since it was about the stupidest thing in the world to deny something somebody saw you do. When he was little, he used to think he could convince people to unsee what they saw, if he just kept denying it. It hadn't worked when he had stood in front of his mom, his fists full of crayons, denying he'd drawn a rainbow on the wall. He had even tried to pin it on Olive, though she was still an infant and couldn't sit up yet. According to Gunter's expression, it didn't seem like denying reality worked any better now than it had then.

"Yeah, you did," Gunter said. "You took my advice and spit in the mask."

"Well," Charlie said, "that was only so I could get a better look at the octopus I found."

"You did not find an octopus," Gunter said.

"Yes, I did," Charlie answered.

"Well, I saw a whale," Gunter said, looking over Charlie's head.

Charlie was well aware that when Gunter couldn't meet his eye he was lying. He also knew Gunter would go to his grave before he admitted it.

"That's nice," Charlie said.

• • •

As he waited for his turn to get on the dinghy back to the boat, Charlie poked around the beach looking for shells, gold doubloons, or the bones of a long-dead pirate.

Out of the corner of his eye, he saw some movement in the palm trees. He looked, but there was nothing. He noticed it again a few minutes later while he was kneeling and looking at some driftwood. He kept his head down and slowly turned his eyes toward the movement. A pair of eyes and the outline of a dark suit peeked from behind a palm tree.

Charlie froze. It was one of the men who had been chasing the van. How was that possible? Why were they here? How did they even get here? They had to have a boat hidden on another side of the island.

It was one thing to chase the captain down a dock in Miami. But somehow, they had followed the captain to

this remote location in the Bahamas. What did they want? What could be so important that they would go to so much trouble?

Charlie got a sinking feeling. Whatever they were after, it was serious. Nobody followed a person this far over some little misunderstanding.

Charlie glanced at Gunter. His next-door neighbor was applying Band-Aids to the cuts and scrapes on Cinderalla's legs from when she had been thrashing around near coral. Gunter hadn't seen the man.

Charlie casually stood up and wandered toward the tree line, pretending he was still looking for shells. He peeked up and saw a patch of dark material disappear behind a tree.

Charlie sped up. The man turned and ran.

Charlie broke into a sprint. A hundred yards ahead, the man was leaping from behind tree to tree.

"Hey," Charlie called. "I can see you. Who are you? What do you want?"

The man didn't answer, but now that he knew he was spotted he stopped trying to hide. Charlie watched as the man in the dark suit, legs pumping, ran deeper into the jungle and disappeared.

Charlie thought about following him, but scenarios rolled through his head of being lost in the jungle and the dinghy leaving without him, and then his dad trying to bargain down the price of a rescue operation. He could see his dad sticking with steely resolve to a bargain-basement fee while Charlie lived on coconuts and drew large SOS signs in the sand for a few months.

He turned back and nearly ran into Gunter.

"What are you doing here?" Charlie asked. "You're supposed to be bandaging up Cinderalla."

"I couldn't take the secondhand smoke," Gunter said. "What are *you* doing here?"

"Nothing," Charlie answered.

Gunter folded his arms. "Nothing but following one of those guys in suits," Gunter said.

"So what if I was?" Charlie said, brushing by him and heading back toward the beach.

"The captain is in deep," Gunter said.

"Deep into what?" Charlie asked over his shoulder.

Gunter didn't answer. Charlie was certain that Gunter didn't know any better than he did.

As Charlie came to the edge of the tree line, he spotted a piece of paper lying on the sand. He casually bent over, scooped it up, and put it in his pocket.

"What is it?" Gunter said, catching up to him. "What did you find?"

"Nothing," Charlie said. "I just don't like to see trash lying around a tropical paradise."

"Give it up, Pennypacker," Gunter said. "You know I will haunt you until you show it to me. I'll follow you everywhere. I'll tell your mom you were mean to Olive. I'll tell your dad you've been ordering expensive movies on his credit card. I'll break in and search your cabin. I'll tell the twins you've been begging to learn Cucuchara. I'll tell Olive that you've ruined things between her and Jimmy Jenkins. I'll tell Claire that you're planning to sneak up behind her and cut her hair. Hashtag: she'll strangle you."

Charlie did not doubt that Gunter would do all those things, and probably some things he hadn't bothered to mention. He sighed. "I get to read it first."

Gunter shrugged. Charlie pulled out the scrap of paper. All it said was:

Take MANTHI with you.
The boss.

It *had* to have fallen out of the man's pocket. A piece of paper would not last twenty-four hours in this environment. It was some kind of clue, but what did it mean?

Gunter grabbed the note and read it, then nodded knowingly.

"Don't even try," Charlie said. "You have no idea what it means."

Gunter handed Charlie the note back. "Maybe not, but I'll figure it out before you do."

Charlie didn't answer. Whatever there was to figure out, he had to do it before Gunter did. His dad could *not* get wind of any of this.

. . .

After everyone had been safely transferred back to the ship, Captain Wisner came on the loudspeaker. "Well, well, folks,

I guess you have a story to take home with you, courtesy of Wisney Cruises. Ha ha. But seriously, any cruise line in the world might have run into a similar situation. Assuming there is a six-year-old who keeps throwing meat into shark-infested waters. Could've happened to anybody who was six and had access to cold cuts and was not being properly supervised, but everybody's back on board with all their original body parts, so lesson learned. Now folks, kick back and enjoy the afternoon. We will soon be underway. We will overnight in Nassau where you will feel free to disembark and experience first-rate dining and exciting nightlife. There's even a casino if you care to try your hand with Lady Luck. In the morning, we will be on our way to the heart of the Caribbean—first stop, Eleuthera. Over and out!"

Charlie was lying on a deck chair next to his dad. "I don't suppose we'll be first-rate dining this evening," he said.

"First-rate burgers or chicken," his dad answered.

Charlie sighed. "Let me guess," he said. "Burger King or KFC."

"And McDonald's or Popeyes," his dad said. "A virtual cornucopia of choice. I will only mention that I have coupons for a particular dining establishment that starts with an *M*."

"McDonald's it is, then," Charlie said. "And I suppose gambling is out?"

Mr. Pennypacker snorted. "Son, if there was any possible way to double my money by throwing around some dice, I'd speed off this boat like the Road Runner. Nobody wins at a casino except the owners. Occasionally they let a little old lady win a hundred dollars, but then they rob her in the parking lot to get it back. That's how *they* get you to believe you could win, too."

Gunter threw himself into the chair on the other side of Charlie. "I'm going to splurge tonight. I have twenty dollars," Gunter said.

Charlie cringed. Spending a lot on food was one of his dad's chief gripes. As he always said, "In the end, what happens to all that expensive food? It goes right down the same toilet as all the cheap food."

"Don't be ridiculous, Gunter," Mr. Pennypacker said. "Do you really think I'd let you go off on your own? What if you didn't come back? That would be thirty dollars a day down the drain."

Mr. Pennypacker paused, then said, "But since you have twenty dollars burning a hole in your pocket, the Value Meals are on you."

. . .

Hours later, Charlie was in his cabin listening to his mom negotiate with Olive about what she would wear that evening. Olive was set on her green "If History Repeats Itself, I'm Getting a Dinosaur" T-shirt and her rainbow-colored My Little Pony skirt. Mrs. Pennypacker was set on anything that matched.

Charlie stared at the note he had found on the beach.

> Take MANTHI with you.
> The boss.

He had been thinking about it all afternoon. He couldn't help it. He knew that was exactly what Gunter was doing, too. Gunter would have written out a copy and been in his own cabin staring at it.

The note could just mean what it said—one of the men was named Manthi and their boss wrote them the note. In a mystery, it would be a red herring—something that only looked like a clue. But if it *wasn't* a red herring, then it had some meaning that Charlie couldn't figure out because he was missing key information. Or else it could be a code.

He was getting more and more convinced that it had to

mean something. If it didn't, why had the guy carried it around in his pocket? Why take it with him all the way to the Bahamas? His mom left him notes like that all the time, usually along the lines of: "Clean your room, it smells like a battalion of unwashed soldiers live there. Love, Mom." He didn't carry those notes around with him, he just stuffed them in the bottom of the trash can and pretended he'd never seen them.

If it was some kind of code, the first thing to do was spot something that looked like repetition, or something that looked out of place. There was no repetition. There was nothing out of place.

He paused. Except that MANTHI was capitalized. Why would the guy's name be capitalized?

Usually, a whole word would be capitalized to signal that it was the main point of the message.

So, MANTHI was the point. Maybe MANTHI was an anagram.

Charlie tore the blank back page off *A Bloody History of Caribbean Pirates* and grabbed a pen from his bag. He ran up to the deck so that he could work without listening to Olive's ten-thousand reasons why her clothes matched, even though her mother swore they didn't.

He sat on a deck chair, careful that it was one of the sturdier ones, and started to play around with the letters.

Manthi. Tan him. Than mi. Am thin. Mat hin. Tim han. Tin ham. Him ant. Him tan. Ham tin.

Or . . . oh no . . . *Hit man.*

Chapter Seven

Hit man? Charlie dropped the paper. It fluttered to the deck. The breeze picked it up, and he grabbed it before it blew over the side.

Hit man. *Manthi* was an anagram for *hit man*. Could that really be right? Was he letting his imagination run wild?

The note was signed "The boss." At first, Charlie hadn't thought that was weird. His dad's boss always said things like "Just keep the boss in the loop," like he was talking about another person.

But if *hit man* was right, then *boss* might mean . . . the capo, the don, the crime boss.

"Trying to figure out what it means?"

Charlie jumped. Gunter had come out of nowhere, like he usually did. The guy was a panther.

Gunter snatched the paper from his hands. He read it and snorted. "Hit man. Like Captain Wisner would have gotten himself involved with the Mafia. Totally ridiculous, Pennypacker."

"Uh-huh," Charlie said. "The note is signed 'the boss,' as in 'crime boss.'"

"Wisner and the mob? I don't think so."

Gunter paused, and then his eyes widened. "Wait a minute. The captain called one of them a wise guy. When we were at the dock in Miami, he shouted, 'Not today, wise guy.' Wise guys are in the Mafia."

"And," Charlie said, "one of them said, 'Nobody avoids us forever.' It's the kind of thing the mob is known for."

"The captain and the mob," Gunter said softly. "How did that old galoot get himself involved with those characters?"

"I don't know," Charlie said. "But it isn't just the captain involved. They've seen *me* see *them* in the jungle. I'm a witness. The mob hates witnesses," Charlie said.

"Bad luck, Pennypacker. They'll try to rub you out," Gunter said. "Getting rid of witnesses is one of the main things they do."

"Well, maybe they'll try to rub you out, too," Charlie said. "That guy probably didn't get a good look at me, so they'll just be looking for a boy, and we're the same height. They might even rub you out instead of me in a tragic case of mistaken identity."

Gunter looked as if he would answer, but then looked away. They were both silent, contemplating being rubbed out by the mob.

Charlie thought about telling his parents. He had no doubt that his dad would demand being taken back to Miami immediately. The problem was, his dad would want to get back to Miami in a hurry so he could file a lawsuit. A lawsuit would enrage the mob. They'd end up in deeper than they already were.

No, that wouldn't work. Somehow, Charlie would have to figure out how to get out of this alone.

At the thought of going head-to-head with the Mafia by himself, Charlie felt a thousand light fingers run up his spine. He had zero experience with the criminal underbelly. He glanced at Gunter. Gunter was the only other person who knew what was going on. And he was pretty wily and would do anything to win. If anybody could help him, it was probably Gunter.

But still, working with Gunter Hwang?

It went against all his instincts, but he didn't see that he had any other choice.

"I feel like," Charlie began, "we better work together to get ourselves out of this and stay alive." He held up a hand, in case Gunter was leaping to the conclusion that he wanted to be friends again. "Obviously, just for this emergency."

"Obviously," Gunter said. "Once we get the mob off our backs, it's business as usual."

"We should enter into a formal agreement," Charlie said. "Otherwise we'll constantly have to worry about double crosses."

"*I* wouldn't worry about double crosses," Gunter said. "You can hardly manage a cross, much less a double."

"Whatever," Charlie said. "I'll write it. My mom makes ironclad agreements—I've heard about a million of them over dinner." He turned his paper to the blank side and wrote:

The parties to this agreement, hereafter known as Pennypacker and Hwang, agree to cooperate to save their lives. This cooperation shall consist of: sharing information, making plans, and conducting operations. This agreement prohibits: double crosses, saving only yourself, and stupid competitions that have nothing to do with the mob. The term of the agreement is from this day, August 18, to the day it is acknowledged by both parties that their lives are no longer in danger. They will then return to their natural state of disagreement about everything on the planet.

Charlie signed it and passed it to Gunter. Gunter read it over and tried to haggle over the legality of the language, but Mrs. Pennypacker was a lawyer and Gunter's parents owned a car dealership, so he didn't get very far. The only edit Charlie made was to add "forthwith" after "everything on the planet."

"Now," Charlie said, "we have to come up with a plan."

. . .

By the time the boat had approached the harbor at Nassau, he and Gunter had settled on the most likely thing to do first. They would get on the Wi-Fi at McDonald's and see if they could find out anything about the captain. Maybe they could discover a clue about what he did to get in deep with the mob. While they were at it, they would also Google "one weird trick to outwit the Mafia" and "staying alive when the Mafia wants you dead" and "little known secrets for evading the mob." Charlie made sure his phone was charged, as Gunter's had been smashed when Cankelton had thrown his bag over the rails.

It was dusk, and the lights of Nassau began to switch on, forming long slivers of silver-blue reflection on the water. Charlie had expected it to be a small town, but it looked as busy as New York. They had stopped at a fueling station to fill up the tanks and now they were headed to the Seaview Marina, where they would dock for the night.

The *Aladdin's Dream* passed under the shadow of two cruise ships, and Charlie felt as though he were looking up at skyscrapers. He felt a pang of disappointment. They should be on one of those ships right now. Charlie should be exhausted from the AquaDuck and buffet-dining on shrimp and orange sodas. Instead, he'd get a taxi to McDonald's with Gunter Hwang and use the Wi-Fi to try to save themselves from the mob. Even getting a taxi might be wishful thinking. For all he knew, his dad might have gotten hold of a bus schedule.

At least scrambling for information on the Wi-Fi would distract Gunter from noticing the rules for ordering at McDonald's. The Pennypackers did not supersize, but they were free to refill sodas, and pocketing extra salt and pepper packets was encouraged. Sometimes, his dad even brought a couple of ziplock bags to fill with take-home ketchup, straws, and napkins.

Charlie could see the sign for the marina straight ahead. There was a long dock and a row of slips, some with boats in them and some empty.

Gunter grabbed Charlie's arm and pulled him down to a crouch below the rail. "There they are again."

"Where?" Charlie asked.

"Right there," Gunter said, pointing.

Charlie squinted. Gunter was right. The men had been standing behind some kind of shed. Now they had stepped out and were marching down the dock to meet the incoming boat. They must have guessed the captain would overnight in Nassau. The *Aladdin's Dream* was a sitting duck.

The boat, which had been idling forward, suddenly jerked back. Charlie crashed to the deck.

"The captain has spotted them," Gunter whispered.

Charlie glared up at him from the floor, "You think so?"

The boat throttled into reverse and began backing out of the harbor.

"Wisner," one of the men shouted from the end of the dock, "We WILL catch up to you! We always do. Nobody escapes our net!"

Captain Wisner turned the boat around. Charlie scrambled up and ran with Gunter to the stern.

The men jumped onto a small inflatable dinghy. One of them yanked the starter and the other threw off the rope attached to the dock. The dinghy roared to life and took off, heading toward the *Aladdin's Dream*.

"What are they going to do?" Gunter asked. "Try to board us like pirates?"

"If they catch up to us," Charlie said, looking around for a weapon, "we'll have to fight them off. We can't let them board or it's over."

"We'll hit them with deck chairs," Gunter answered.

The *Aladdin's Dream* pulled farther ahead of the dinghy.

One of the men in the dinghy shouted, but not at the

Aladdin's Dream. He was wildly pointing at an incoming cruise ship.

The dinghy disappeared behind a Princess Cruise liner.

The boys silently watched the mammoth ship pass by.

"Do you suppose they got run over?" Gunter said hopefully.

Charlie crossed his fingers as the Princess Cruise ship slowly continued on its way to port.

The ship passed the spot where the men had been. Charlie squinted. The dinghy popped up and bounced on the waves of the ship's wake.

The arms of two suit jackets emerged over the side of the rubber boat and the men appeared. They clutched at each other as they rode up and over the waves.

Charlie sighed. "They got wet, but they didn't get run over."

"They're probably enraged," Gunter said.

"At least we've gotten away from them. For now," Charlie said.

"For now."

Charlie's dad staggered up the stairs. "What was that," he asked. "Why did we jerk around like that? Why are we heading away from Nassau?"

"Uh," Charlie mumbled, "I'm not sure."

As the boat plunged into darkness and the lights of Nassau grew distant, Charlie heard the loudspeaker crackle.

"Sorry about that!" the captain said in his usual overly cheerful voice. "Sadly folks, we've just been informed that Nassau is experiencing an outbreak of cholera. We will want to stay well clear of that fiasco! Nothing ruins a vacation faster than fighting over the bathroom, running out of toilet paper, and writhing in agony. Could those bigger cruise ships do an about-face so fast? No, they could not. But here on Wisney Cruises, when I hear *cholera*, I throw this boat in reverse and get my guests the heck out of there. I hear *waterborne disease* and I say, I won't stand for it!"

There was a long silence, as if the captain was allowing the idea of fighting over the bathroom and running out of toilet paper to sink in. Then he said, "Folks, all this schedule change means is that we shall arrive at Eleuthera, which is cholera-free, sooner than expected. We'll go full speed ahead and drift outside the island's reef until daylight. The moment, the very instant I can see where I'm going and not crash us into razor-sharp coral, we are cruising straight for the closest dock. Now, Chef Mickey will be heading down to the galley to whip up one of his astounding dinners. Remember when you're eating that astounding dinner that you'll be able to keep it down because you don't have cholera. Bon appétit!"

"Cholera?" his dad said. "That is a serious disease. And with Olive only six, what might have happened if I had laid out the extra money for a real Disney cruise? We'd be heading straight for disaster. Well! I'd better get downstairs and discuss this with your mother. Congratulations to me will be in order."

Mr. Pennypacker practically skipped to the stairs.

"No getting on the Wi-Fi at McDonalds, so that plan is out," Gunter said.

"If we can't find out about the captain on the internet, we'll have to interrogate him. We have to know exactly what he did to get the mob on his tail in the first place," Charlie said.

"The captain loves to answer questions, just not the ones you asked," Gunter said, snorting. "You'll be off the bridge before you know it, none the wiser. He's told me how deep the ocean is at least ten times over the years, including yesterday."

"Wait," Charlie said, "you went to talk to him?"

"So what if I did?" Gunter asked. "I've known him longer than you have and I guess I don't have to report my every move to you. There are a lot of things I do that you don't know anything about."

"We signed an agreement," Charlie said.

"It was before the agreement," Gunter said.

"I went to talk to him before the agreement, too," Charlie admitted.

"What is a knot?" Gunter mimicked. "Are sharks dangerous? How far are we from Miami?"

"Exactly!" Charlie said.

"He's a crafty old codger," Gunter said. "We might be able to crack him, but I'd need a good cop."

"What?"

"I'd need a good cop for my bad cop. That's how the coppers get people to admit their crimes. One guy is all mean and then the other guy pretends he wants to help but he can't unless he knows the truth."

"Why shouldn't I be the bad cop and *you* be the good cop?"

"Now you're just stretching all the limits of reality," Gunter said. "You can't be a convincing bad cop. I'm the only one that can look like I've gone rogue."

Charlie didn't see why Gunter seemed proud of that fact, but he couldn't really argue against it.

"When should we talk to him?" Charlie asked.

"How about now?"

Chapter Eight

Captain Wisner was leaning back in his chair, just like Charlie had last left him, except without the cup of coffee. As far as Charlie could tell, driving a boat was mainly just sitting around, putting it on autopilot and then occasionally throwing it into reverse when you noticed the Mafia waiting for you.

Gunter had silently crept in behind the captain. He leaned close to his ear and whispered, "We have a few questions for you, Captain Wisner."

The captain jumped, and Charlie stepped onto the bridge. "That's right," he said. "Just a few friendly questions."

"My questions might not be that friendly," Gunter said.

"That guy," Charlie said, hooking a thumb at Gunter, "has gone totally rogue. But I'm different. All I want to do is help you to help yourself. Which I can do if I know the truth."

"I may be inclined to get at the truth in a more sinister way," Gunter said darkly.

"Look at you," the captain cried. "Two friends! Well of course it's the most natural thing in the world for two boys of the same age to strike up a friendship."

"We're not friends," Gunter said.

"Not friends," Charlie confirmed.

The captain looked puzzled, but quickly recovered himself. "Not friends it is, then! And yes, I can see you want

answers. Hold on to your hats, here they come: Looking for a very deep swimming pool? The Bahamas are home to a blue hole six hundred and sixty-three feet deep. Fancy a stop at Cat Island? If you went for the cats, prepare for disappointment. The island was named for pirate Arthur Catt. Still wondering about cholera? It's a bacterial disease. Millions of cases every year. Good sanitation is the key to prevention. Those sharks that were so interested in sandwiches? Blacktip reef sharks. They're known as somewhat retiring, personality-wise. But then, throw some sandwiches in the water and look what happens.

"Captain," Gunter said, interrupting his torrent of answers to questions nobody asked.

Captain Wisner leaned forward and pressed a button. A loud bell echoed throughout the ship. "Dinner gong!" the captain cried. "Off you go. Don't keep Chef Mickey waiting." Captain Wisner hustled them to the door and shoved them out. "Chefs are notoriously temperamental, you know. They say cooking is an art form. True? Not true? A question for the ages!"

Captain Wisner slammed the door shut, turned the lock, and pulled down the shade.

"What just happened?" Charlie asked.

"We got bamboozled by the old devil," Gunter said. "That's what happened."

. . .

Chef Mickey appeared to have a deep love for eggs. They'd had egg sandwiches for breakfast and now had a choice of egg salad or an omelet for dinner. They hadn't had anything but eggs since a hot dog the first night and the sandwich morsel on the beach. Olive stared down at her omelet and said, "Why is that Mickey Mouser killing so many baby birds?"

"I don't know," Charlie said. "But don't complain about it."

"I can complain if I want to."

"I know you can, but don't," Charlie said. "Everybody is still blaming you for the sharks."

"I'm six, I can't be blamed," Olive said proudly, as if the defense that her mother had floated on the beach could be trotted out for any and all occasions.

"They're not blaming you out loud," Charlie said, "but everybody is secretly blaming you. They're blaming you in their minds."

"In their minds?" Olive said softly.

Charlie guessed this might have been the first moment that it had occurred to Olive that other people had thoughts she didn't know about.

Olive jumped up and stood on her chair. She shouted, "Stop blaming me in your minds!"

Mrs. Pennypacker's head snapped up, always on the alert for incoming meltdowns. Charlie shook his head to let her know it was a false alarm and pulled his sister down from her podium.

"I'm gonna keep blaming you in my mind," Gunter said to Olive.

The twins pointed at Olive and screeched.

Claire giggled and said, "Hashtag: Blaming!"

"Everybody stop talking!" Olive said.

Cinderalla slid into a chair and looked glumly at her egg salad. She picked up a limp dill pickle and said, "Livin' the high life."

Gunter leaned across the table and said, "We didn't dock at Nassau because those same guys were there. How come they're after the captain? What did he do?"

Cinderalla shrugged and took a bite of pickle. She grimaced like she'd never tasted one before.

Olive said, "I know, right? Who even invented pickles? Why?"

Charlie decided to try the good cop strategy. "Listen, Cinderalla, I want to help you. I can't help you unless I know the truth."

Cinderalla laid down her pickle and looked Charlie straight in the eye. "You want to help me, do you? How about you get me off this tin can and onto Norwegian Cruise Line as a beloved lounge singer? And hey, if you want to be a regular Santa Claus, how 'bout you set me up a retirement fund so I'm not workin' a job like this when I'm ninety?"

"He don't got a lot of money," Olive said, hooking her thumb at Charlie. "My dad only gives him five dollars a week, and sometimes I go in his room and take some. But only the new quarters because they're shiny. I got a whole collection of shiny quarters."

Charlie whipped his head around to his sister. "I *knew* you were stealing from me. I *knew* it was you."

"I guess the cat's out of the bag on that one," Cinderalla said.

Olive shrugged. "I can't be blamed," she said.

"You can too be blamed," Charlie said. Then he paused. He was getting off track. Olive's thievery would have to wait.

"Seriously," he said to Cinderalla, "what did the captain do to make those guys so mad?"

"Yeah," Gunter said. "We can do this the easy way or we can do this the hard way, but I want answers."

Cinderalla reached over and squeezed Gunter's cheeks together, making his lips pop out like a duck's bill. "What do you want?" she asked him.

Gunter attempted to speak, but Charlie couldn't really understand him through the duck bill.

"Hey, you could smack him," Olive said to Cinderalla. "I'll say it was me 'cause I can't be blamed."

Cinderalla paused to consider Olive's generous offer. Then she let go of Gunter and went to smoke near the porthole.

"I don't think she knows anything," Gunter said, rubbing his face.

"Probably not," Charlie said. "I had another idea, though. There might be things happening when everybody is asleep. Cinderalla might not know anything, but other people might be part of whatever is going on. If we sleep on deck, we might overhear a secret meeting or see somebody doing something suspicious."

"Could be," Gunter said. "It might even be a guest. We can't rule anybody out."

"We don't have 'sleeping on deck' in the agreement, so we'll have to add a rider."

"What's a rider?"

"An amendment to the agreement," Charlie said. He usually didn't listen to his mom when she went off on her lawyer stories, but he must have been around it so much that it had just seeped into his brain. He even sounded like a lawyer.

"Why do we need a rider?" Gunter asked.

"Because we'll be on the deck overnight and anything could happen. What if a rogue wave takes me over the side? I need to have it in writing that you'll pull me out and not just give me a thumbs-up as I drift into the darkness."

Gunter snorted. It was exactly the kind of thing the guy would find funny.

"I'm telling mommy that you're gonna sleep outside," Olive said. "I bet you're not allowed."

Charlie silently swore. He'd forgotten she was there. He would have to go to the nuclear option to keep her quiet. He had helped Olive hide many, many crimes and had kept a strict record of them for future use.

He leaned over to his sister and said softly, "If you tell, I will tell mom about the glass figurine you broke, the cabinet handle you broke, the remote control you broke, the toilet you broke when you flushed down a handful of Shopkins because you wanted them to swim in waves. Oh, and the sheets that have magic marker all over them that I helped you hide in the back of your closet."

Olive considered this list of unexplained mysteries that had occurred in the Pennypacker household. In a guttural, demon-like voice, she said, "I will cook you like a French fry."

"Uh-huh," Charlie said. "But you won't tell."

. . .

The captain finally dropped the anchor after ten o'clock. Charlie had been checking since eight, waiting for the captain to turn the boat over to Mickey Mouser for night watch. The crew took shifts when the boat was anchored, to make sure they didn't accidentally float away and wake up just as coral was ripping through the hull and the boat was sinking like the *Titanic*.

Charlie took his blanket and a water bottle up on deck. He planned to put together a makeshift bed on one of the sturdier deck chairs. Gunter was right behind him. He glanced at Charlie's blanket and water, then went below and brought up a bottle of water and two blankets.

Charlie sighed. He guessed the two blankets were supposed to be superior to his one blanket. Even a simple thing like what to bring on deck was a competition for Gunter Hwang. If Kyle were there, he would have just asked Charlie ahead of time what he should bring and would have congratulated Charlie on his foresight and planning.

Charlie paused. If he really thought about it, Kyle would have been too scared to sleep on deck. As great a friend as Kyle was, he was kind of a worrier. Kyle was still convinced that there was a beehive somewhere in Charlie's house, because he had seen a bee in the kitchen last year. Every time he came over, Charlie saw him scan each room, listening for telltale buzzing. If Kyle were informed that the mob was after him, he might spontaneously combust.

The deck was eerily dark. The moon had passed behind the clouds, and it was hard to see where the railings were. Charlie thought the only way he would even know he was on a boat was the gentle rocking of the waves and the quiet splashing of water against the hull. He shivered at the thought of accidentally going over the side. He would plunge into the inky water and be dragged away by the current. Rider or no, he really had to wonder how fast Gunter would throw him a rope or sound the alarm. Charlie imagined the lights on the boat drifting farther away until they disappeared and he was alone, waiting for some nightmare beast to rise from the deep and cut him in half. All that would be left of him would be his wallet floating along with the current, eventually found by a retired couple walking their dog on the beach.

Gunter shoved his arm. "What are you doing?" he asked.

"Thinking about what it would be like to go overboard," Charlie said quietly.

"That wasn't the plan," Gunter said, "but if you're determined, it's your funeral. Enjoy your swim."

"We should watch both sides of the boat," Charlie said, ignoring Gunter's snide remark. "I'll take starboard and you take port."

"Maybe I should take starboard," Gunter said.

"Does it really matter?" Charlie asked.

"No, not really," Gunter said.

Charlie lay carefully on his deck chair, listening for ripping fabric before he put his whole weight on it. He settled in and gazed up at the stars. With the boat in darkness, it looked as if the sky had somehow lowered itself. Like the stars were way closer than they usually were.

He could just see the lights of Eleuthera in the distance and could hear the waves rolling over the reef. He'd never heard of Eleuthera, so maybe the Mafia wouldn't even know where it was. After all, they weren't exactly a seafaring people—gritty backstreets were their neighborhood, not the Caribbean.

"How's Kyle?" Gunter said from across the deck.

Charlie stiffened. Why was Gunter Hwang asking about *his* friend Kyle? "He's fine," he said.

There was a long silence. Charlie felt like he was expected to say something back. "Who are you hanging out with these days?"

"A lot of people and nobody in particular," Gunter said. "My dad says Americans are jerks and you have to keep them at arm's length."

"*You're* American," Charlie said.

"I'm half Korean, which is the part my dad focuses on. My mom focuses on the German half. Neither of them focus on the American part."

"Why does he think Americans are jerks?" Charlie asked. He shouldn't have been surprised; Charlie had always felt Mr. Hwang looked down on him. Especially since Mr. Hwang had once looked down at Charlie and said, "You are not as good as my son. At anything."

"I don't know," Gunter said. "Just jerky stuff he's heard about."

Jerky stuff he'd heard about? Charlie got a sinking feeling that some of the jerky stuff Mr. Hwang had heard about had to do with him. Mr. Hwang would only have heard Gunter's side, which would have been filled with outlandish exaggerations to make Gunter look like a blameless angel. Maybe he should write a letter to Mr. Hwang to set the record straight.

But why should he care what Mr. Hwang thought?

Mr. Hwang had paid Mr. Pennypacker thirty dollars a day to pawn off Gunter. Mr. Hwang's opinions should mean nothing to Charlie.

Still, bringing up anything that had to do with why he and Gunter weren't friends anymore gave him a queasy feeling.

Charlie rolled over and tried to sleep, but Mr. Hwang and his hatred of Americans kept surfacing in his mind like a buoy in steep waves.

Chapter Nine

Charlie had dozed on and off. Sleeping on deck had been a bust. It was uncomfortable, and he had not seen or heard anything. Now it was just before dawn; the sky was not yet pink, but the stars had gone. Charlie stretched.

He heard footsteps across the deck. Charlie pulled the blanket over his head and peeked out.

The captain was jogging up the steps to the bridge with a cup of coffee in his hand. He passed a staggering Mickey Mouser. No wonder Mickey's food was so terrible—the guy never had time to sleep.

After the door to the bridge closed behind the captain and Mickey Mouser had gone down the stairs, Charlie threw off his blanket and stood up. Gunter was still asleep, which

Charlie was glad about. He really did not want to have any more conversations that started with "How's Kyle?" He could work with Gunter, but it had to be all business. There was no reason why they should have conversations about their personal lives. Or the past. Or who was friends with who.

The island was straight ahead. It looked very long, but not wide. Then, Charlie noticed they weren't the only boat waiting for sunrise. There was a small sailboat to their left, and a bright blue vessel, twice the size of the *Aladdin's Dream*, on their right. The hulking ship was named the *Sea Wind*.

"That boat is huge. It must have rich people on it," Gunter said.

Charlie jumped. The guy was a cat! Just when you thought you knew where he was, he turned up somewhere else without a sound.

"They're probably one-percenters—they have so much money they just throw it at anything," Gunter said.

"Yup," Charlie said. "They probably have to pay ten thousand dollars a day."

"Hey, maybe I could tell your dad that your mom made reservations on it, just to see if he would faint."

Charlie snorted before he could stop himself. Years ago,

they'd had a game called "Make Mr. Pennypacker Fall Down," consisting solely of telling Charlie's dad about ways he could lose all his money.

"Wait a minute," Gunter said, pushing past him. "Did you see that?"

"What?" Charlie asked.

He pointed at the *Sea Wind*. "That."

Charlie looked over at the *Sea Wind*. The mobsters. They stood at the rails, staring intently at the *Aladdin's Dream*.

"Uh-oh," Charlie said. "I bet that boat is owned by the crime boss!"

As he said it, more and more people appeared on the deck of the massive boat and looked over the rails. They were dressed in shorts and T-shirts and looked nothing like mobsters. All of them were peering at the island. It was only the men in suits staring at the *Aladdin's Dream*.

"No," Gunter said. "They bought tickets. That's a ferry."

"We better tell the captain," Charlie said. "And this time, we demand answers."

Before Charlie could demand answers, the door to the bridge opened. The captain stood at the top of the stairs, staring at the *Sea Wind*.

The men ducked out of sight. The captain shook his fist

in the air, went back to the bridge, and slammed the door shut.

"And one . . . two . . . three," Gunter said, counting on his fingers.

At three, the engines roared on and the anchor came up with a clatter. The boat reversed and turned toward the open sea.

Charlie looked back at the *Sea Wind*. The men in suits stood up again. Charlie could just make out their furious expressions as the captain pushed the throttle and steered the boat away from land.

"Let's go have a chat with the captain," he said.

Charlie tried the door to the bridge. It was locked. He knocked on it but there was no answer. "Captain, we know you're in there and we know who those men are. We know you're on the run. Open up, we demand answers."

"Sorry," the captain said, "I can't hear through this locked door."

"You *can* hear us," Gunter said, "or you wouldn't have answered us."

"What?" the captain said.

"He can't stay in there forever," Charlie said. "Sooner or later he'll have to tell us what's going on."

The sun began to rise as the *Aladdin's Dream* sped away

from the island of Eleuthera and the ferry headed toward it. They had bought some time, but Charlie was not so sure how much time. It didn't look like those guys were going to give up easily.

Charlie smelled the familiar scent of frying eggs coming from the galley and made his way below deck. The corridor was crowded with passengers still in their pajamas, asking each other questions.

"I can see right out of my porthole that we're going away from an island, not toward it."

"Why? Where are we going?"

The loudspeaker crackled. "Good morning, good morning, good morning, folks! It's another beautiful day in the Caribbean! What a fun-filled day we have in store for . . . wait! What's that? It can't be! Folks, I'm getting an emergency transmission up here. There has been a military coup on the island of Eleuthera. Armed rebels have taken over. Well, I say, I won't have any part of that! When I hear *military coup*, I say 'not on my watch.' We here at Wisney Cruises are committed to fun, and if there is anything fun about a military coup, I would like to know about it. No, folks, we are steering well clear of that. We shall chart our course to the Turks and Caicos, which is fantastically coup-free. Enjoy your eggs!"

"Did you hear that?" Mr. Pennypacker asked his wife. "A military coup. Think what might have happened! That big boat that was next to us is heading right into it. Exactly like we would have been if we were on some oversized Disney ship. Whew! We are nimble!"

Mrs. Pennypacker didn't answer. She knew only too well that the military coup would go right on the list of why not spending money was wise.

Other passengers did not seem as convinced of imminent danger as Mr. Pennypacker.

"First cholera, now a military coup?"

"What kind of operation is this?"

"I just wonder what's next."

Charlie wondered the very same thing. What next?

. . .

At breakfast, the military coup faded as a topic when a protest was launched by Jimmy Jenkins's parents over the egg situation. They claimed their young son was losing weight because of the absence of cereal, and Mickey Mouser was forced to produce a box of Cap'n Crunch. This was met with a round of applause. Poor Jimmy probably wished he never complained about the eggs after Olive launched herself at his face and then informed him that they would kiss and have cereal together for the rest of their lives.

The budding romance, or hostage situation, was interrupted by the loudspeaker. Captain Wisner came on and said, "Crew meeting on the bridge in five, over and out."

"Crew meeting," Gunter said.

"Exactly," Charlie said. "That's how we'll get some real information."

"We'll sneak up there and hear everything they talk about when they think nobody is listening," Gunter said.

"Yup," Charlie said. "And if any of them are in league with the captain, we'll find out about it."

Olive turned from Jimmy and said to Charlie, "I get to come to the crew meeting, too. I have to be included in everything. Mommy said so."

"She did not," Charlie answered.

"Take me or I'll cook you like a French fry and not get blamed."

Charlie stared at his sister. The whole "I can't be blamed" idea was bringing out the worst in her. Since she had a lot of worst to bring out, somebody was bound to get hurt. Jimmy Jenkins took the opportunity to slide down his seat and disappear under the table.

"You're not cooking anybody," Gunter said to Olive.

"Maybe I can't do it," Olive said, "because I'm not allowed to use the stove, but the evil witch from Sleeping Beauty can. Her name is Maleficent and she does what I say. *That's* how I won't get blamed."

"Your sister is creepy," Gunter said.

"Yes. Yes, she is," Charlie answered.

Olive's eyes widened at this betrayal of family loyalty. She said, "You're gonna be in big trouble, Charlie. I'm telling and you *will* get blamed."

As Olive began a diatribe of all the ways that Charlie would be punished for suggesting she was creepy, most of which involved serious physical injury, Gunter stood up and said to Charlie, "Well? Are you coming? Because I'm going."

Charlie glanced at Olive, who had just mentioned ordering sharks to tear him to pieces. Jimmy Jenkins sobbed under the table.

Charlie was definitely going.

. . .

Charlie and Gunter passed Claire taking a selfie in front of the Elsie and Annie cabin. "Hashtag: girls on vacay."

The twins nearly knocked Charlie over as they marched down the hall, having a heated debate in their mother tongue.

Cinderalla and Micky Mouser strode toward them, and Charlie pretended to admire the drawing of Don Ducky. Gunter leaned against the wall and hummed a tune.

"What do you suppose the old heathen wants now?" Cinderalla asked as she passed by them.

"Probably wants to tell me that he sent all my money to the House of Pancakes, so my girlfriend can have more pancakes while she curses my name. She's as thin as a rail, but you can never fill her up!"

"Did anybody ever tell you you're a drama queen?" Cinderalla asked.

Cinderalla and Mickey Mouser disappeared up the stairs.

Gunter pressed his index finger over his lips, and they tiptoed forward, leaving Claire and the twins behind.

The voices coming from the bridge were faint and then grew louder and clearer as they climbed the stairs. The door was shut and the shade drawn. Charlie and Gunter crept up to it and pressed their ears against the metal.

"What do you mean, walk there?" Cinderalla asked from behind the closed door to the bridge. "Why can't they just get a taxi?"

"No taxis," Captain Wisner said. "The booking says I provide one free excursion per port, but I have to keep the costs down."

"Well, so far you haven't made it to *any* port, so that's kind of beside the point. Plus, this is the stupidest excursion I've ever heard of," Cinderalla said. "How did I ever get involved in this operation?"

"I believe," the captain said, "you got involved in this operation shortly after you were fired from Norwegian Cruise Line. Spending all your time sunbathing, drinking piña coladas, and telling guests you were a beloved lounge singer instead of cleaning the cabins was always going to end badly."

"Did you send all my money to the House of Pancakes?" Mickey asked.

"Once again," the captain said, "no, Fred, I did not send your salary to the House of Pancakes or any other nationwide chain specializing in breakfast. I suppose I should inquire why you keep asking me that?"

"Because you can't fill her up," Mickey whispered desperately. "Not ever."

"I have to get out of this costume," Cankelton said. "I don't even look like a cricket."

There was a long silence. Then the captain said, "We've got to pull it together. Just a few more trips like this and I am back on track."

"But the antennae keep falling in my face. I feel like I'm getting hit with spaghetti. What am I supposed to do about that?"

"I'll lend you a hair clip," Cinderalla said to Cankelton. "Cap, some of the kids keep asking me why those men were chasing you down the dock in Miami," she said. "You know, those two guys in suits. I've been wondering that myself, actually. And then they say those two guys were at Nassau, too."

"I know which two guys in suits, but which kids are asking?" the captain asked.

Charlie and Gunter looked at each other. Even though they had attempted to interrogate the captain, it somehow didn't seem like a good idea for the captain to know that they had been asking Cinderalla questions.

Chapter Ten

"The two older boys are the ones asking questions," Cinderalla said. "One of them has that nightmare little sister that has an opinion on everything."

"Shark girl," Cankelton said. "And, Cap, didn't I say you can't mess with guys like that?"

"The two boys," the captain said in a thoughtful tone. "Well, at least it's not the twins. They have their own secret language, but they won't teach it to you even if you beg. Who knows what they talk about."

"I'm cutting off these wings. Nobody expects me to fly anywhere anyway," Cankelton said.

"I don't even like kids," Cinderalla said. "And here I am, pretending to be a delightful princess for their enjoyment. Who was *my* princess when I was a kid? Why didn't *I* get a fairy godmother?"

"She can never be filled up," Mickey said. "There aren't enough pancakes in the whole world. Where will it end?"

"Everybody," the captain said loudly, "stop wallowing in your own personal nightmares. If I want to wallow in nightmares I conveniently have enough of my own. Let's get back on topic. Myra, according to my map, it will take you less than half an hour to walk the guests to the excursion. Now, be ready to depart at ten sharp tomorrow morning. Cankelton, keep doing whatever it is you do on this boat. I assume at some point I will discover what it is. All of you, don't forget you're supposed to throw around some Disney-like sentiments when you're with the guests."

"Like what?" Cinderalla asked.

"I don't know!" the captain said. "Believe. Or something like that."

"Believe what?" Cinderalla asked.

"Believe in . . . miracles, or fairies, or something," the captain said.

"I believe I'm ill-treated," Cankelton said.

"And Fred, cut it out with the eggs. I heard there was

practically a mutiny just to get some cereal. I bought cereal because everybody in the whole world likes cereal."

Fred, or Mickey Mouser as he was more commonly known, was finally jolted out of his morose House of Pancakes musings. "I am a chef," he said. "Serving Lucky Charms and Cap'n Crunch will not get me any closer to a Michelin star. I might have been able to do something interesting with Shredded Wheat, but I suppose we'll never know. Tomorrow's breakfast will be scrambled eggs, and let's see if the six-year-old she-devil or her crybaby boyfriend complain about it."

Captain Wisner let out a long and protracted sigh. "Whatever," he said. "All right, gang, back to work."

Charlie motioned to Gunter and they slipped down the stairs ahead of Captain Wisner's crew. Charlie pointed to a bulkhead, and they hid behind it.

Cankelton climbed down the stairs, his antennae gently slapping his face as he trudged past them. Cinderalla and Mickey Mouser came down together and paused at the bottom. Charlie leaned forward to listen.

"Why don't you just dump her?" Cinderalla said. "How did you ever get yourself involved with Madam Pancakes anyway?"

Mickey adjusted his ears and said, "It crept up on me all slow-like. I was the chef at Mr. Luigi's Cottage of Spaghetti, and she started coming in and ordering two or three plates at

a time. Naturally, I was flattered. At first, I'd go out to dinner with her and she'd finish hers and start working on mine and I thought it was great that my girlfriend didn't live on salads. Then she started insisting that we only go to all-you-can-eat buffets. Then we had to go early and stay late. She actually got banned from Panda King; they said she ate enough fried rice to feed a province in China. The cook was having a nervous breakdown—he couldn't shake those Woks fast enough! Then, I started noticing that no matter how much food I brought into the apartment, it seemed to vanish overnight. I even tried an experiment once: I left a ten-pound bag of potatoes on the kitchen counter. It was gone the next morning." Mickey's voice dropped to a whisper, "Who eats ten pounds of potatoes overnight?"

"I guess *she* does," Cinderalla said. "She was supposed to be my second stewardess and play Minnie to your Mickey. Now I'm stuck cleaning all those cabins by myself and you're half of a team. Why did she storm off the boat the morning we were leaving?"

Mickey ran a hand through his hair, knocking his mouse ears back around his neck. "I caught her in the galley. She was heating up a pan full of butter and six dozen eggs were on the counter. I said, for the love of all that's holy—see a doctor. She threw an egg at me and said she was going to the House of Pancakes."

Cinderalla snorted. "And I thought my love life was bad. I'm going to my cabin. I know I'm supposed to go back to the mess hall, but I've been Olive Pennypackered enough for one morning."

Charlie winced. His sister had become a verb.

Cinderalla and Mickey walked across the deck and disappeared down the stairs.

"The coast is clear," Gunter said. "Now we do a debriefing. We have to go over everything we've heard and figure out what we've learned from this spying mission."

"Obviously," Charlie said.

"Good," Gunter said.

"Good," Charlie answered back. "I don't think we heard anything that will tell us what the captain did to make the Mafia mad, but every clue could be important later on. What we know is that Cinderalla is Myra and Mickey is Fred and there really is a girlfriend that can't stop eating, cause unknown."

"Right," Gunter said. "And we know that we'll be walking somewhere tomorrow morning because the captain wants to keep costs low on the excursions."

"That is, assuming we actually land on the Turks and Caicos, which would be a miracle at this point. If we do make it into a port, we should go on the excursion—they might have Wi-Fi and we've got to see if we can find any information about the captain online."

"Right," Gunter said.

"Okay, so we also know that Myra was fired from Norwegian Cruise Line because she's obsessed with being a lounge singer, Cankelton doesn't like his cricket costume, and not even the captain knows what the guy's job is."

"Cankelton was on all the other trips I took when the boat was the *Kingfisher*," Gunter said. "He always carried the bags on and off but I never saw him otherwise, so I guess the captain has been wondering what he does for years."

"What about when the captain said that after a few more trips like this one he would be back on track? Did he mean a few more Disney-like trips? Why? The characters are terrible."

"But they don't know that," Gunter pointed out. "Remember? Cinderalla described herself as a delightful princess."

"I guess," Charlie said. "Hey, did you notice that the captain totally dodged the question about the men in suits? He turned it around to wanting to know who had been asking."

"He's a slippery one."

"You don't suppose he'll try to make us walk the plank because he thinks we know too much, do you?"

"Well, there's no plank and your parents would probably start asking where we were, so I would say no."

"I meant figuratively," Charlie said, his cheeks flushing.

"He might make Olive walk the plank, though," Gunter said with a snort.

Charlie ignored that comment and said, "Cankelton."

"What about him?" Gunter asked.

"Forget interrogating the captain, he won't tell us anything," Charlie said. "But like you said, Cankelton has been with the captain right back to when it was the *Kingfisher*. He said he warned the captain not to mess with guys like that. He must know they're Mafia. If anybody can tell us why they're after the captain, it's Cankelton."

"Cankelton," Gunter said softly. "We'll just have to get him alone."

"I doubt getting him alone will be the hard part. We've got to find him first. We've got to figure out where he spends his time between meals. He disappears like a ghost."

. . .

They had arrived at the Blue Haven Marina on Provo, Turks and Caicos, at dawn. As the sun crept higher in the sky, Charlie lay in bed, amazed that they had actually landed somewhere. As the man from immigration boarded the boat to stamp all the passports, Charlie wondered how long it would be before the mobsters figured out where they went. It might be a couple of days. The men had gone to Eleuthera on a ferry, not their own boat. Hopefully there was no airport there and they'd have to return on the ferry to Nassau. Then they'd have to figure out where to look for the *Aladdin's Dream* next. Maybe those wise guys had just made a fatal mistake. They'd put themselves so far behind the *Aladdin's Dream* that they might not be able to catch up.

Olive provided a repetitive backdrop to his thoughts as she complained in the adjoining cabin that one hundred of the Dalmatians were still missing. It was her current theory that the dogs had been left behind in Miami and they should go back and get them because they were lost and nobody would feed them. Mrs. Pennypacker was gamely explaining that since everybody loved Dalmatians, they were no doubt eating three square meals a day. Mrs. Pennypacker only hoped they would not get spoiled from all the food and love.

As Charlie thought about the captain's situation, he became more and more convinced that the most important thing he and Gunter had heard the day before was when the captain had said that after a few more trips like this one he would be back on track. It must have some important meaning because it made absolutely no sense. His Disney-like cruise was awful, and he was on the run from the mob. What was going so great about that? How did the captain expect to keep running these trips with the mob on his heels? Did he have a plan to get rid of them? How many passengers could he actually convince that Cinderalla was a charming princess? The Yelp reviews would kill him off faster than the mob. What was going on that Charlie couldn't see?

Cankelton had to be the key. Whatever the captain was up to, Cankelton would know. Charlie and Gunter would just have to force him to spill the beans.

The crackle of the loudspeaker interrupted his thoughts. "Good morning, folks," the captain said, "and what a beautiful morning it is here in the Turks and Caicos. Not a military coup or cholera outbreak in sight. If you will make your way down to the dining room, Chef Mickey is preparing a marvelous breakfast of his world-famous scrambled eggs. Also, cereal *will* be available, no matter what he says. At ten o'clock sharp, you will meet Cinderalla on the aft deck and be off on an exciting excursion. After an invigorating hike where you will view the native flora and fauna, you will experience what few have done before you—a conch safari. That's right, you will view conch of every size and description at an actual conch farm. Would you get this rare opportunity if you were on a bigger ship? No, you would not. There, you would find yourself stuck with zip-lining, kayaking, scuba diving, and shopping. Ho and hum. But here on Wisney Cruises, we are dedicated to taking you off the beaten path. None of your friends have ever visited a conch farm, and none of them ever will. Enjoy your day, over and out!"

A conch farm? What were the chances that a conch farm would have Wi-Fi? They had to see if they could find out anything about the captain. Charlie had heard his mom talk about digging up dirt when she was getting a case ready. He remembered that she always looked at court records to see if the defendant was in the habit of living a life of crime. She also searched social media, hoping to find incriminating posts. One time, she prosecuted a guy for stealing a television, and it was a slam dunk because he'd Instagrammed himself kicking back and watching it. All they had to do was find something like that on the captain and the whole mystery of what he did would unravel. If they knew what he did, they could start coming up with ideas to fix it.

In the dining hall, breakfast was the usual plate of eggs and the usual complaints about eggs. Though the captain had said cereal would be available, Jimmy Jenkins had finished the box of Cap'n Crunch and Mickey Mouser claimed all the other boxes had been attacked by weevils. Charlie began to think that Mickey might want to stop complaining about his girlfriend's obsession with pancakes and start worrying about his own obsession with eggs.

Olive's plate was a layer of ketchup with eggs buried somewhere underneath. "I can't look at all these dead baby birds," she said. "I'm going to tell Maleficent to curse Mickey Mouser and turn him into an egg, and then we'll see how he likes getting cracked open and fried."

Charlie sighed. "What is it with this witch stuff?" he asked. "Why all of a sudden are you so interested in Maleficent?"

Olive laid down her fork and said, "Because she has magical powers. I need magical powers. I'm in charge of her, so now I have magical powers. Duh."

Charlie was tempted to mention that if Olive was so sure she was in charge of a witch, maybe she should tell that witch to bring back the hundred missing Dalmatians. He decided not to when he remembered he'd be debating a six-year-old.

Jimmy Jenkins had crept to the opposite end of the table,

clearly hoping that Olive would not notice the arrival of her elusive fiancé. He had become skilled at dodging his frightening betrothed. Jimmy was assisted by the twins, who threw themselves down at the table and blocked Olive's view while firing back and forth in Cucuchara. They sounded like deranged dolphins.

Claire sat down and stared at her plate of scrambled eggs. She took out her phone and snapped a photo. "Hashtag: sick of eggs," she said.

Charlie guessed Claire lived her whole life on social media. Hashtag: no moment too small. Since they didn't have Wi-Fi on the boat, as soon as they got in range of a signal, Claire's friends would be deluged by hashtags of every thought and meal she'd had.

"What's a conch?" Olive asked.

"I think it's some kind of snail," Charlie said.

"What's a safari?"

"I think it means trip."

"We're going on a snail trip?" Olive asked.

"I guess so."

"Then we won't have to walk very fast," Olive said, and then dissolved into fits of giggles. "Get it? Snails are slow!"

"Got it," Charlie said. Olive repeated her joke four more

times, each time finding it more hilarious than the last. She might not crack up anybody else, but she was an Olympic champion at cracking herself up.

Charlie didn't care about the conch—his only idea at the moment was to get online and get information about the captain. Court records might give him an answer. He knew the mob wouldn't file anything in court—they would avoid the law. But if the captain owed a lot of money to different people, it would back up one of his ideas—the captain was in deep over cash. Then, maybe he could get some answers on how to get out of that kind of mob problem. It was possible that there was some kind of process. The Mafia was a business, after all.

Chapter Eleven

Cinderalla led the group through the marina and out onto Governor's Road. The group was only Charlie, Olive, Gunter, and the twins. Everybody else had decided to stay on the boat. Vendors of every sort had boarded and set up folding tables filled with shells, handmade jewelry, hats, sunglasses, and stacks of T-shirts—it was like a traveling mini-mall. Charlie had left Mr. Pennypacker circling around the wallet in his wife's hand like a cop surveilling a criminal.

Charlie held Olive's sweaty little fist while surreptitiously scanning his phone for a signal. He had argued that Olive should stay on the boat because he was on vacation and shouldn't have to babysit. She had thrown herself on the deck and turned red to win the debate. He had since lectured her on doing exactly what she was told and not running off and not talking too much. She had just looked at him and mouthed the words, "cook you like a French fry."

Cinderalla stared at her map and said, "We take a left and follow this for about three quarters of a mile, then we take a left on Leeward Highway."

"Three quarters of a mile?" Charlie said. He worried he'd be carrying Olive by the half-mile mark. He knew perfectly well that she could walk that far, but his sister took every opportunity to claim that her legs hurt and she needed to be carried.

"Three quarters of a mile," Cinderalla said. "That's what it says on the map."

"Wait a minute," one of the twins said.

The group froze and turned to the twins. Everybody was so used to Cucuchara that it seemed impossible one of them had just spoken English. It was like coming home and finding your dog talking on the phone.

"We're supposed to be going on a hike to see flora and fauna," either Patience or Prudence said. "How are we supposed to see flora and fauna on a regular road?"

Cinderalla shrugged. "How should I know? I'm just a princess leading a tour," she said. "Now, we could stand here all day while the sun burns a hole through the top of our heads and we eventually tip over from dehydration. Or . . . we could start walking."

The twins turned to each other and screeched in Cucuchara. It sounded like they were issuing orders to have Cinderalla thrown into a dungeon and mercilessly tortured. Then, as suddenly as they had started, they stopped. They both pushed their hair behind their ears and smiled. Charlie thought that if there were alien life forms walking among humans, he was pretty sure he knew who they were.

The group trudged down the road while Cinderalla pointed out the interesting flora and fauna. The flora were the trees that lined the side of the road, which she identified as "look over there, trees." The fauna was one mangy dog in

somebody's backyard, correctly identified as "a mangy dog." The flies that followed them down the road were identified as "a waking nightmare." The twins attempted to communicate with the dog in Cucuchara, but it just lunged at the fence.

Gunter grabbed Charlie's phone and checked it. Everything was out of range except a signal in front of the house with the dog, but that one had a password on it. Maybe they'd have better luck at the conch farm.

Olive made a desperate bid to be carried by throwing herself onto a patch of wild grass on the side of the road and claiming she couldn't feel her legs. Charlie, having had time to plan ahead, said, "Maleficent is not going to work for a girl who's too lazy to even walk."

Olive lay there for a minute, searching her mind for a loophole to that theory, gave up, and got up. Charlie handed her a bottle of water from his backpack as a reward for acting like a normal person.

They turned onto the Leeward Highway. It was busier than the road they had been on, mainly with taxis whose drivers seemed incredulous that they'd chosen to walk instead of ride. They beeped their horns, shouted out their windows, and threw their hands up. Cinderalla found the entrance to the conch farm and said, "Cripes, *finally*."

Charlie took his phone back from Gunter and checked it all the way down the drive, but no signal.

Their guides were James and Berna. James was tall and thin and wore a pressed white shirt, black dress slacks, and a thin gold cross around his neck. Berna was a short woman in a wrap skirt and an oversized T-shirt that had a shark riding a surfboard. James gave them a lecture on the queen conch, a sea snail of the Strombidae family. Of the more interesting facts, Charlie learned that a conch had a foot, and when in peril it could hop away. Or at least try to hop away—there was only so fast a creature could go underwater with only one foot. James had shown them the nets offshore where the conch was farmed. Now, they were peering down into aboveground tanks full of queen conchs in various stages of development.

When they reached the tanks full of conchs, Charlie spotted a signal on his phone. While James picked up a large conch from the tank and showed Olive its pink underside, Charlie hopped online.

Gunter leaned over his shoulder as he punched in *Captain Ignatius Wisner*. There was a Facebook page with only one post that said, "Hi, I'm Ignatius." He had six friends who were all probably bots. There was a newspaper article in a local paper that had interviewed small business owners about how they competed with large corporations. The captain was quoted as saying, "If you can't beat 'em, join 'em." His Twitter handle was @SeaDog123. His first tweet was *Captain Ahab was an idiot*. Literature lovers across the globe had flamed him, and he'd gone down in fiery Twitter defeat.

"Geez," Gunter said. "The captain doesn't understand Twitter at all. He threw out bait to wolves and then he writes 'Everybody leave me alone.' Like that was going to happen."

"There's nothing here. Let's try court records." Charlie saw the records were all by county and narrowed it down to Dade. He searched on the captain's name, but it only showed six unpaid parking tickets for the van.

He was coming up empty. The captain was one of those old people that, unlike Claire, did not live their whole lives online. Realizing he wouldn't find anything on the captain, Charlie Googled "how to escape the mob." The top hit was "How to elude the mob if they are trying to kill you." He opened it up. It had 591 views. Who knew there were hundreds of other people trying to escape a hit?

As he read through the article, he felt his stomach drop. A person should pack one bag and then burn their house down so that no clues about their life could be found. They could never contact family and friends again. Ever. They had to become vagabonds in the small towns of the Midwest, taking on jobs for cash, like picking vegetables. But they could never stay anywhere. They had to keep on the move, never getting to know anybody.

"There's no advice on how to actually fix a problem with the mob," Charlie said. "There's only advice on how to keep running away from them."

Charlie's attention was pulled from his phone by Olive asking James, "You're gonna eat them?"

James laughed. "I will not eat them all by myself. We will sell them so other people can eat them. Conch stew is very good. Conch fritters are even better."

Charlie was leery about where the conversation was going. Olive was already fixated on Mickey Mouser killing all the baby birds so they could eat eggs, now James was talking about eating the conch.

"You're gonna eat your own pets," Olive said in a low voice. "How 'bout somebody eats you? I will make my witch cook you up and eat you like a French fry!"

James dropped the conch into the tank and grasped the cross around his neck. "Why do you speak of witchcraft?"

"She's just talking," Charlie said hurriedly. "Don't pay any attention to her, she's only six."

"That's right," Olive whispered, in the kind of low and raspy tone that would make a demon shudder. "I'm only six."

"Really," Charlie said to James, "just ignore her. She tells everybody she's going to fry them."

"*I* won't do it," Olive said. "Maleficent will do it for me. She's my witch and she does what I say."

"Blasphemy," James said, pointing at Olive and backing away.

"I made you say a curse word," Olive said, looking satisfied.

"That's not a curse word," Charlie said. "Cut it out, Olive."

"My witch comes to me in the night," Olive whispered.

"You are possessed," James said. "All the signs are there."

"No, she's not," Charlie said. "She's just awful."

"French . . . fry," Olive whispered and then giggled uncontrollably.

James stared at her, horror etched on his face. He turned and ran.

"Where's he going?" Gunter asked Berna.

Berna, who until this moment had not said one word, chuckled and said, "I expect he's gone to get the pastor."

"A pastor?" Charlie asked, fear beginning to creep through his insides. "Why? Why does anybody need a pastor at a conch farm?"

Berna leaned against the water tank and said, "A pastor can hold down the demon for the exorcism. If you believe in possession, what you have here is a textbook case. This should be good."

"Exorcism?!" Charlie cried.

"What's an excorism?" Olive asked. "Is that another curse word?"

"Crap," Cinderalla said.

"I know *crap* is a bad word. My mommy said so!"

"How far away is this pastor?" Cinderalla asked, looking around.

"He's right next door," Berna said. "You can see the steeple from here."

Charlie turned. There it was, a white steeple poking above the palm trees.

"We should probably go," Cinderalla said.

Charlie grabbed Olive and made her drop the conch she had planned to release back into the wild. Down at the beach, James was already coming back with a shorter man, who huffed and puffed to keep up with him. The man wore a large silver cross over his starched shirt and clutched at it.

"Ah," Berna said, "that man coming back with James has been looking for a demon his whole life. He's always ranting about them—they're behind every corner, they're hanging from the trees, they're hiding in your house. He says he's gonna drive them out, but he's never been able to catch one for all his preaching. You are about to make his day, little one. He'll finally have something to show for all his talk."

"She's not a demon!" Charlie said. "Not a real one, anyway."

"I know that. I can see with my own eyes that she's just a bad-tempered little girl, but try telling *him* that," Berna answered, hooking a thumb at the pastor.

"I'm not bad-tempered!" Olive shouted, as if she could shriek her way to being amiable.

"Run," Cinderalla said. She tucked her costume into her jeans and sprinted away. Charlie dragged Olive as fast as he could make her go. To inspire her to move faster, he told her the men were coming for all the Shopkins in her pockets. This seemed to breathe fire into Olive's short legs and they caught up to Cinderalla.

On the Leeward Highway, Charlie said, "We'll never be able to run all the way back to the marina. Maybe we should hide in the woods."

"No," Cinderalla said. "There's a taxi." She wildly waved, and the taxi slowed to stop a few feet ahead of them.

"We won't all fit," Charlie pointed out.

"We don't all need to fit," Cinderalla said. She shoved a ten-dollar bill into Charlie's hand. "Just get her out of here!"

"There they are," James shouted at them from the opposite end of the drive. "Hurry, man," he called to the huffing and puffing pastor.

"Go, go, go," Cinderalla said, pushing Charlie and Olive toward the taxi. Olive, usually resistant to anything she was being forced to do, climbed in quietly, seemingly aware that she had taken the "cook you like a French fry" gambit a step too far.

Cinderalla told the driver to take them to the Blue Haven Marina. As the taxi pulled away, she turned and faced the pastor. "Back off, brother."

Chapter Twelve

At the marina, Charlie paid the driver and dragged Olive onto the boat. He looked for his parents on deck and in the mess hall, then he finally found them in their cabin. His mom was surrounded by her purchases. His dad was holding up a hand mirror framed by sea shells. "Ten dollars for shells that are just lying around free in the sand? It's madness."

"No," Mrs. Pennypacker said cheerfully. "It's a souvenir."

Mr. Pennypacker's tallying of money down the drain was interrupted by Charlie's explanation of why they were back from the excursion so soon.

"Olive," Mrs. Pennypacker said, "why would you ever, ever say you would cook someone like a French fry?"

Olive stared at the alarmingly large Dalmatian on the wall of the cabin and said, "I can't be blamed."

"Well," Charlie said to his mom and dad, "I'll leave you alone to hear the convoluted explanation of why she can't be blamed and how the evil witch will help her with her French-frying dreams."

Olive looked at Charlie like, if she really could fry him, she would be turning the burners on.

"Thank you, Charlie, for bringing her home safely," Mrs. Pennypacker said. She turned to Olive and said, "Madam, it seems we have a lot to talk about."

Charlie left them to it and climbed up to the deck. He leaned against the railing and saw Cinderalla in the distance, speed-walking ahead of Gunter and the twins.

When she was a hundred yards from the boat, Cinderalla yelled, "Captain, we got a problem. Time to shove off."

In the distance, James turned the corner into the marina.

Captain Wisner leaned out the window of the bridge. "The suits again?" he asked Cinderalla.

"No," Cinderalla said. "The tour guide at the conch farm thinks Olive Pennypacker is possessed by a demon."

"Holy Rice-A-Roni," the captain muttered. "And the worst of it is, he's probably right."

Cinderalla raced up the gangplank. "Hurry up," she called to the rest of the group following her.

Far behind James, his pastor staggered along. Charlie squinted. Two more men suddenly appeared behind the pastor. The men in suits had just turned into the drive. They were about a hundred yards behind the pastor and gaining on him.

How? How had they caught up to them so fast?

"A preacher *and* the suits?" The captain said to Cinderalla. "Remind me not to take up gambling—Lady Luck hates my guts."

Gunter broke into a sprint. The twins shouted something in Cucuchara and followed him.

Unlike the other times that the mob had showed up, this time there were adults on deck to see them. Charlie wondered if he'd have to tell his parents what was really going on.

The twins' mother grabbed Cinderalla's arm and said, "What in heaven's name is happening? Who are all those people and why are my daughters running from them?"

"Olive Pennypacker is happening," Cinderalla said.

Much to Charlie's surprise, this appeared to be a perfectly logical explanation.

"Who are those men?" Jimmy Jenkins's dad demanded.

"That would be James," Cinderalla said, "our tour guide at the conch farm. His out-of-shape friend is a pastor determined to drive the demon out of Olive Pennypacker. I say, good luck with that."

"What about those other men? The two in suits?" Jimmy's dad asked.

Cinderalla shrugged. "They're not *my* friends. Ask the captain."

Gunter and the twins boarded. Cankelton had appeared from nowhere and pulled up the gangplank. Maybe, just maybe, they would have time to get away.

The captain and Cankelton had the boat unmoored in seconds. This time, though, it did not drift away from the dock. The current had been in the captain's favor in Miami, but it ran against him today.

Cinderalla and Cankelton tried using the oars from the dinghy to push off while the captain started the engine, but the boat would not be moved.

James reached the dock. He paced back and forth, appearing leery of approaching the young witch's vessel alone. He held his cross and shouted over his shoulder to his friend, "Run! Can't you run?"

The pastor had slowed to a walk, heaving in breaths with each step.

The men in suits had not slowed to a walk. They were in a full-out sprint and had passed the churchman, seeming determined to end this Caribbean game of cat and mouse.

The engines roared on and the captain began to edge the boat away from the dock.

The men in suits reached the end of the pier. They were close enough that Charlie could see their faces. The tall one was consumed with fury, the shorter one had descended into madness. He threw his briefcase on the ground and then stomped on it for good measure.

The *Aladdin's Dream* edged out a few more feet. The tall one shouted, "That's it! I have had it!" He dropped his briefcase and ran back down the dock. Then he turned around and took off at a sprint toward the boat.

Charlie grabbed Gunter's arm. "He's going to try to jump." Charlie and Gunter picked up deck chairs, ready to use them as weapons.

The man made a flying leap. He smashed into the side of the boat and slid down into the water, like Wile E. Coyote failing to make it across a canyon.

Charlie and Gunter dropped the chairs, ran to the railing, and looked over the side.

As the boat drifted farther away, the man flailed in the water, his nose bleeding.

"Wow, he looks mad," Gunter said.

The man's partner threw him a rope and began hauling him back to shore as the boat turned toward open sea.

Charlie heard the adults chattering behind them. What is going on? Why did that man just fling himself into the water? Why didn't we pick him up? Why are we leaving so soon?

Various theories were floated, including another military coup, or skipping out on the bill at the conch farm.

Captain Wisner hit the throttle, and they went full speed ahead out of the marina.

Gunter said, "What do you suppose the captain will say now that everybody has seen those guys?"

"I don't know," Charlie said. "But something about this doesn't add up. Why didn't they shoot at us? Don't they have guns in those briefcases?"

"Too many witnesses," Gunter said. "What would be the chances of them hitting all of us, plus James and his friend the pastor?"

"Maybe," Charlie said. "Or maybe the crime boss gave them specific instructions. Maybe they're supposed to put cement boots on the captain and throw him overboard. You know, to send a message."

"Send a message to who?" Gunter asked.

"I don't know," Charlie said. "I think it's just something they do, like, 'look what happened to the guy who crossed us.'

"Oh, right."

"Folks!" the loudspeaker blared. "My apologies for the rushed departure from the Turks and Caicos! Once again, it seems our own Olive-tsunami has stirred things up. Claiming to be a witch is frowned upon here. Would Wisney Cruises allow a beloved child to go to jail? And as far-fetched as it seems, she is probably beloved by *somebody*. When I think jail, I think no, sir, not my witch and not on my watch."

"Jail?" Charlie said.

"Yes, folks, when I see a conch farm tour guide, a religious-type fellow, and two executives from the ministry of culture, I think jail time for whoever insulted the country's dignity. Your bigger cruise lines might allow a six-year-old to waste away in the slammer, but I won't have it. Sit back and enjoy the sunshine, folks, secure in the knowledge that imprisonment is *out* and sun and fun are *in*. We barrel straight ahead to our next destination, which will be . . . our next port."

Jimmy Jenkins's parents debated what Olive could have done to merit jail time. His father did not believe that a six-year-old could commit a serious crime. Mrs. Jenkins was firm in her opinion that you couldn't put anything past Olive Pennypacker. As Charlie had seen no sign of his parents on deck, he assumed they remained down below with the now notorious Olive Pennypacker.

Charlie said, "The ministry of culture. He's creative, I'll give him that."

"He doesn't even know where we're going," Gunter said.

"That's the last straw," Charlie said. "If there is any strategy to get away from those guys, we have to know what the captain did in the first place. The only person who might be able to tell us anything is Cankelton. If it's about money, maybe we can figure out how to raise it to settle the debt. We could do a GoFundMe page. I mean, it has to be money? Right?"

"It could have been anything," Gunter said. "The captain might have bad-mouthed Italian Americans. My dad says bad things about Italian Americans all the time."

"Your dad says bad things about all kinds of Americans all the time," Charlie pointed out.

"There goes Cankelton," Gunter said, pointing at the insect as he trudged toward the stairs.

"Let's go," Charlie said.

They casually strolled past Mr. and Mrs. Jenkins, who had pulled the twins' mom into a discussion of Olive Pennypacker. As it turned out, she had taken to calling Olive "Voldemort's daughter." Jimmy Jenkins kept tugging on his dad's sleeve, saying, "This means I don't have to marry her, right? Right? Dad, right?"

Cankelton had reached the bottom of the stairs, and instead of going left toward the cabins, he turned right toward the mess hall, or the stately dining room, as the captain liked to call it.

Charlie and Gunter ran down the stairs. Cankelton passed through a narrow door at the end of the corridor.

They raced to it and Charlie slowly turned the rusty handle. It made a rasping sound. He and Gunter froze, listening. There was no sound from the other side of the door. He gently pushed on it.

The door swung open with a squeaky whine into a long and dimly lit corridor. The air was cool and smelled like sea salt and Windex. Either side of the walkway was lined with deep shelves that ran floor to ceiling and had high sides so supplies wouldn't fall out in rough seas. One side of the shelves was stocked with cleaning products, cans of paint, coiled rope, and marine equipment. The other side was filled with canned goods and a row of what appeared to be perfectly good boxes of cereal. At the end of the corridor, light seeped out from the sides of a badly fitted metal door.

Charlie tiptoed toward it with Gunter right behind him, breathing in his ear. He put one eye up to the crack.

The room was large, much bigger than his parents' cabin.

It appeared to have been decorated by a madman from the 1960s. A lava lamp cast shadows on the walls, which were covered with hand-painted signs. The lettering on the signs was expert, but they all said the same thing: SANCTUARY. There were no chairs, but large pillows were strewn on the lime-green shag carpet that covered the floor. Cankelton's bed appeared to be a large black velvet couch. Cankelton was still in his insect costume, lounging on the couch.

Gunter leaned over his shoulder to look inside. "What the . . . ?"

Cankelton sat up. "Who's there?" he asked. "This is private quarters. Go away."

Charlie pushed the door open. "It's us, Cankelton. And we have a few questions for you."

Chapter Thirteen

Cankelton jumped up from the couch and paced the room, the legs on his costume swinging in every direction. In between telling them to go away he accused them of mutiny, pretended to call the Coast Guard, and claimed the boat had sprung a leak and so they'd better go find life jackets. When those gambits didn't pay off, he sneezed and swore he was coming down with the bubonic plague from a recent rat bite.

Charlie made himself comfortable on the velvet couch. "We want answers and we'll stay here until we get them. We're done messing around."

"You can't stay here!" Cankelton said, brushing his antennae away from his face. "This is my sanctuary."

"I'll say," Gunter said, looking around at the signs covering the walls. "You've got quite the setup. What exactly do you do on this boat? Just hang out here all day?"

"I don't have to tell you anything," Cankelton said.

"Absolutely not," Charlie said, "as long as you don't mind having us around."

Cankelton wrung his hands and said, "I don't like company!"

"Then you'd better tell us everything you know," Gunter said. "What did the captain do to make those guys in suits so mad?"

"What guys? Which guys? I don't know!" Cankelton said. "How should I know? I'm always down here. The captain does stuff to make people mad all the time. It's his main thing— he drives people nuts."

"No answers," Charlie said, crossing his arms, "no leaving. Sooner or later, my parents will get worried. We'll be reported missing. Then the boat will be searched. Then you'll have everybody in here."

"Everybody?" Cankelton muttered, pacing back and forth. "All those people in my sanctuary?"

"Everybody crowded into your sanctuary," Gunter said. "I wonder if they would all even fit? It'll be wall-to-wall people."

Cankelton looked distraught and unnerved, which made

Charlie wonder if he'd been the one to paint the dwarves in his cabin. He'd probably been told to think up new dwarves and looked inward for inspiration.

"I can't have more people in my sanctuary! I don't like people in my sanctuary." Cankelton jogged over to the corner of the room and picked up a handheld radio. He pressed a button and said, "Captain, captain, Cankelton," and took his finger off.

"Captain here, over," Captain Wisner said in a crackling voice.

"Captain," Cankelton said, "I got some guests here asking questions you told me not to answer. Will you speak to them, sir?"

"All right," the captain said. "Where are they? Over."

"In my sanctuary," Cankelton cried.

"Where?"

"I mean, my cabin," Cankelton said.

"Your cabin?" the captain asked. "I thought you slept under a table in the mess hall. Over."

"That was only the first night, ten years ago."

"Where the heck is your cabin?"

"At the end of the supply closet. Hurry! Over, over, over!"

There was a long pause, then the captain said, "The end

of the supply closet? Really. Right, I'll be down as soon as I can put us on autopilot. Over and out."

Cankelton laid down the radio.

"The captain didn't even know where you stayed?" Gunter said. "How come he doesn't know what you do on his boat or even where you sleep?"

Cankelton wrung his hands. "Stop badgering me with questions!"

"Well?" Charlie asked. It wasn't an answer he needed to help solve the mystery of the men in suits, but he was beginning to be fascinated by the mysterious Cankelton.

"All right!" Cankelton said. "I'm the captain's brother-in-law. My wife pressured him to give me the job, as she don't like me hanging around the house. Or hanging around any town she's in. It wasn't ever specified exactly what the job was, so I took my own initiative and decided to load and unload the bags. Course, I ran out of initiative after that. Initiative will only take you so far, in my experience. Then I found this room. Oh yes, it was full of junk when I found it," Cankelton said wistfully. "But I got it cleared out fast enough. Little by little, I brought in my flea market finds. Now, nothing makes me happier than puttering around my sanctuary. It's like I've gone back to the days when I dropped out of college and joined a commune. Except I'm not communing with anybody and I think I'm becoming a hermit. There. That's all of it."

"And you don't know anything at all about those guys who are chasing the captain?" Gunter said.

"I try not to know things," Cankelton said. "If I know something I shouldn't know, then I just unknow it. The only thing I haven't been able to unknow is that I've been miserable since this whole Disney-like thing started. Used to be I could wait until everybody was asleep and go make a sandwich, nobody the wiser. All the sudden, I'm forced to eat with the guests. I hate guests! And on top of that, I have to wear this ridiculous getup. Look at me! I don't have any peace anymore. I'm an insect without peace."

"But why?" Charlie said. "Why did the captain start running this Disney-like disaster? Does it have anything to do with those men? Gunter said the fishing trips used to be great. It doesn't make sense why the captain changed to this."

"Fishing trips. Those were the days," Cankelton said softly. "I'd load the last bag, then creep down here until the trip was over. Good times."

The door flew open and Captain Wisner charged in. He came to a sudden stop as he took in the room. "A lava lamp on my boat," he said softly. "You're kidding me."

The captain noticed Charlie and Gunter. "Well, it's you two. Cankelton, why didn't you say? These boys have questions and I have the answers! How deep is the deepest part of the ocean? How—"

Charlie put his hand up. "No, captain," he said forcefully. "You are not going to throw an avalanche of questions and answers at us."

"That's right," Gunter said, going behind the captain. He closed the door, turned the key, and put it in his pocket. "This time, we ask the questions."

"Of course, you can ask questions," the captain said in his too cheerful voice. "Just not at this moment because I've got to be up on the bridge making an important announcement. But I shall see you soon!"

Captain Wisner made a run for the door, pushing Gunter out of the way. He tugged on the doorknob. "It's locked. Where's the key, Cankelton?"

Cankelton had curled up on a corner of the couch, not even bothering to brush the antennae out of his eyes. "The key was in the lock," he whispered. "Now there are people locked in my sanctuary. People are supposed to be locked *out* of my sanctuary."

"All right kids, ha ha, very funny. Now, really, give me the key," the captain said, sweat running down the sides of his face.

"I don't have it," Gunter said, shrugging.

"I don't have it, either," Charlie said. "And that key will never, ever be found unless you answer our questions."

"Never, ever," Cankelton said with a sob.

"Those men in suits were not from the ministry of culture," Charlie said. "They were the same guys that have been chasing you since Miami."

"The ministry of culture," the captain said, "if there is one, would have been very dismayed at today's events. What was your sister thinking of, going around pretending to be a witch?"

Charlie was about to explain that Olive had only claimed to *know* a witch, but then he

realized the captain was trying to steer him off track. The man was a magician at getting a person off a subject.

"Get out of my sanctuary," Cankelton whispered.

"We know you're on the run from the mob," Charlie said. "What we want to know is *why*."

"The mob? What mob?" the captain said. "No, the thing to focus on is that here we are, in the beautiful Turks and Caicos. That's what everybody should be thinking about."

"We've just *escaped out of* the beautiful Turks and Caicos," Gunter said. "Just like we did from Miami, Nassau, and Eleuthera."

"That's right," Charlie said. "And we've kept things quiet for you. I haven't told my parents anything I've seen. Our silence has worked to your benefit, but we're not going to keep quiet anymore unless you tell us everything."

The captain crumpled onto the couch next to Cankelton. "You want to know everything about my upcoming demise, do you? Came to see the old captain say hello to Davey Jones's Locker? Planned to watch this boat become as scarce as the *Flying Dutchman*? If it amuses you to watch this old sailor fail himself, fail his fellow captains, and fail the long and august history of seafaring, well, go right ahead. The jig is up anyhow."

"What jig?" Charlie asked. As usual with the captain, Charlie had become a little confused. He wasn't sure what the *Flying Dutchman* or Davey Jones's Locker were or what they had to do with anything.

"The jig is up on this whole operation," the captain said. "It's taking on water fast and will sink, sooner rather than later."

Gunter glanced at Charlie and shrugged. "I think you better tell us the whole story," he said.

"The whole story, with nothing left out," Charlie said. "And nothing added in like how deep the ocean is."

"You want the whole, sad story, do you?" the captain asked.

"Sad, sad story," Cankelton murmured.

"We'll be the judge of whether it's sad or not," Gunter said.

"Very well," the captain said. "Prepare yourself for sadness. As Gunter knows all too well, this boat used to be the *Kingfisher*. I chartered fishing trips, and fine trips they were. Those were the days, eh, Gunter? Fishing all day long and eating the catch for dinner."

"It was fantastic," Gunter said.

"Fantastic," the captain said. "All except my finances. My finances were not fantastic, they were a fiasco! Sure, you and your dad loved practically having the boat to yourselves, but

I was going broke running two or three cabins down to the Caribbean. This boat needs to be full to turn a profit!"

"Going broke," Gunter said.

"I knew it," Charlie said. "I knew it was money."

"So you borrowed money from the mob and now you can't pay it back." Gunter said. He turned to Charlie. "I've been thinking about it and I'm pretty sure they'll just break his kneecaps. They probably don't kill people for owing money or they'd never get their money back."

"What if they wanted to break *our* kneecaps, too?" Charlie asked.

"I don't see why they would—we don't owe them money."

"Don't be ridiculous," the captain said. "If somebody was going to break my kneecaps just because I owed them money, I'd need a hundred extra kneecaps just to get started."

"We're not talking about everybody you owe money to," Charlie said. "We're talking about those two mobsters who have been chasing you all over the Caribbean."

"Mobsters from Harvard Law, more like it," the captain said. "I *wish* all I had to worry about was a crime family, heh, Cankelton?"

"Why would mobsters go to Harvard Law?" Charlie asked.

The captain waved his hands in a dismissive gesture.

"Forget the mobsters. If you're not careful, you'll end up the kind of people who think extraterrestrials are in charge of the government and President Kennedy is still alive and living in Aruba." The captain snorted. "Mobsters. That's a good one."

"Seriously, Captain. Are you actually trying to deny those guys are mobsters?" Gunter asked.

"Forget it. We've seen too much. We're on to you," Charlie said. "I found a note that said 'take Manthi with you.' *Manthi* is an anagram for *hit man*. And it was signed by 'the boss,' as in crime boss."

"Yeah, Cap," Gunter said. "We have the evidence."

The captain stared at them as if they were speaking in Cucuchara. "You found a note, which was conveniently an anagram? And then suddenly I'm on the run from the mob?"

"Exactly," Charlie said. As he said it, he paused. Hearing it out loud, it didn't sound like a mountain of evidence.

"They aren't mobsters," the captain said. "They're lawyers."

Charlie snorted. "They're not lawyers."

"Not just any lawyers," the captain said. "Disney lawyers."

Charlie and Gunter glanced at each other. "Lawyers?" Gunter said.

"Mr. Flynn and his partner Mr. Manthi, or, as you like to

call them, Mr. Hit Men, Esquires," the captain said. "They've got some beef about my cruises. I say, balderdash! I was meticulous in changing the details. Everywhere you look, it's not exactly the same—Cinderalla, Mickey Mouser with an *r*, Snowed White, one Dalmatian."

"Lawyers?" Charlie cried.

The captain nodded. Cankelton whispered, *"Disney* lawyers."

That was not possible. Had he and Gunter spent the last few days on the run from lawyers? They had even signed an agreement! They had been working together to save their lives because they were about to get rubbed out.

Charlie paused. It had been the note that had really convinced him that those guys were from the mob. Though, when he had considered what the note might mean, one of the options had been that it meant nothing. It was a red herring.

He'd fallen for a red herring. Charlie felt his face flush as red as it had been the time he'd run out to the car after dark in his underwear to get his homework out of the back seat and set off the Henderson's new crazy security system. When a siren went off and lights illuminated him on the driveway, he had stood there weakly waving to everybody in the neighborhood who had come out to look.

"Are you kidding me?" Charlie said. "You're on the run from lawyers? Why not go on the run from the Dalai Lama? Maybe we could worry that we were about to be killed by Santa Claus or the Pope? Who goes on the run from lawyers? My own mom is a lawyer."

The captain paced the cabin. "You don't understand, son. They're *Disney* lawyers! They're the Leviathans of the legal field. They're Supermen, without the Kryptonite problem. They're Yodas, only taller. They're Captain Marvels without the shazam. They're Spidermen, weaving a web of motions and petitions. They are ruthless purveyors of ceases and desists."

"Really?" Gunter said. "We figured the mob was going to put you in cement shoes. Are Disney lawyers *that* kind of ruthless?"

"Worse!" the captain said. "If somebody put me in cement shoes and I found myself sinking like a stone to Poseidon's lair, I might still have a chance. A friendly dolphin might come along and nose me to a buoy. A whale shark might give me a ride. A mermaid might decide I was handsome. All long shots, but they could happen. Nobody has *any* shot with a Disney lawyer! Their papers are deadlier than a great white, they'll sting you like a box jelly, they'll sink their teeth into you like a moray eel, and they'll roll you like a saltwater croc."

Charlie folded his arms. Lawyers. They had been on the run from lawyers. It was ridiculous, no matter what the captain said about moray eels and saltwater crocs.

"They've been trying to serve me papers for a month," the captain said. He sighed and shrugged his shoulders. "I suppose it doesn't matter. It's all up with me now. The renowned Captain Ignatius Wisner is about to go down with his ship. Long may he rest."

The captain looked defeated. It occurred to Charlie that the whole Disney-like gambit wasn't just to rip off cheap tourists like his dad, but was an act of desperation from a very desperate sea captain.

"Well," Gunter said, "at least we're not in any danger of dying."

"Don't count on it," the captain muttered.

"Wait. What did you say? What do you mean, don't count on it?" Charlie asked.

Chapter Fourteen

"Don't count on it means, my boy, that we left the TC so fast that we didn't get fuel," the captain said. "On top of that, we didn't properly exit with immigration. How are we supposed to arrive anywhere else if, according to the passports, we've never left Turks and Caicos? Not that we have enough fuel to get anywhere else. And, I may have gone a little skimpy on the marine radio front—the range is not what it could be should one wish to call the Coast Guard after one has drained the fuel tanks. I'm over a barrel! I only have enough fuel to get back to the TC, but if I go there, those danged lawyers will pounce on me!"

"You're low on fuel?" Charlie asked.

"But why didn't you get fuel at the marina?" Gunter cried.

"That was the plan!" the captain said. "I thought I had

all the time in the world and, also, I may have accidently taken a nap. Those lawyers weren't supposed to figure out that I'd gone to Provo; it was off my usual route. Somehow, they figured it out. Then they were poking around the marinas, spotted the hullabaloo on the road with that danged pastor, and followed everybody back to the boat. Dodging Disney lawyers is hard enough, but how was I to know that I'd get Pennypackered?"

Charlie winced. Olive's exploits were dragging down the whole family's reputation.

"So we are floating somewhere off the Turks and Caicos with not enough fuel to get anywhere else," Charlie said. "We're not on the run from the mob, but we are on the run from Disney lawyers. And if we don't get our passports stamped as exiting the TC, we'll be on the run from immigration officials, too," Charlie said.

"That's about the size of it," the captain said. "Welcome to Wisney Cruises."

"And when you say your marine radio is not great at calling the Coast Guard, exactly how bad is it?" Gunter asked.

"Might as well be shouting into the wind."

Cankelton rocked himself back and forth. "Get out," he whispered.

"You don't have any choice, then," Charlie said. "You'll just have to go back and face them. Anyway, it's not our problem. Though thanks for letting us live in terror all this time, thinking we were on a hit list."

"I can't help your bizarre imaginations!" the captain cried. "And, I will just point out, it is more your problem than you think. Do you imagine those lawyers will let your parents off scot free? Your father knew this wasn't a real Disney cruise. I clearly explained, on AbsolutelyWayCheapestCheapestCaribbeanVacationsCheapestImACheapskate.com, that it was Disney-like only. My whole pitch was 'why pay through the nose when your kids won't even notice the difference?' As far as the lawyers will see it, everybody who bought tickets participated in the fraud. They'll take him for all he's got."

Charlie froze. Gunter shrugged and said, "My dad wasn't even here and I don't see what anybody has on Mr. Pennypacker. He's just cheap. Really cheap."

"They'll get him for being an accessory to the crime," Charlie said softly. He knew from his mom that a lot of innocent, or nearly innocent, or hoping they were innocent, people got swept up in crimes as an accessory. If his dad got sued for all his money, their life at home would descend into madness. They'd probably sell the house and start camping in the woods. Mr. Pennypacker would teach them how to hunt and gather for dinner—pizza would be out and squirrel would be in. They'd huddle around a campfire through the long winter. They'd be wearing clothes made out of tree bark and take baths in a stream.

They would never, ever go on vacation again. The Pennypackers would spend the rest of their lives on one long holiday in the forest.

Cankelton's sanctuary was silent. The captain alternated between sighing and narrowing his eyes at the lava lamp.

Charlie paused. Why was he giving up so easily in the face of lawyers? He had been willing to take on the mob and now he was making plans to move to the woods without a fight.

"Okay, so we're low on fuel and have a useless radio. If we go back to Turks and Caicos to get our passports stamped and fill up the tank, this vacation will come to a screeching halt and we'll all end up in court," Charlie said.

"There's no way out of this mess," the captain said. "Nobody outfoxes a Disney lawyer."

"We'll see about that," Charlie said.

"We will?" Gunter asked.

"We will," Charlie said. "The first thing we have to do is

get back to the Turks and Caicos, get fuel, and get our passports stamped."

"Manthi and Flynn will be there," Gunter pointed out. "What will we do about them?"

"Right," Charlie said. "They'll be there looking for the *Aladdin's Dream*, that's the key. We have to make sure it's impossible to find the *Aladdin's Dream*. Look at all these pictures," Charlie said, waving his hand around at the Sanctuary signs. If you've been wondering what Cankelton's good at—"

"Many times," the captain said.

"He's good at lettering," Charlie said. "It's like he knows every font on the internet. He can repaint the name. He can put it back to the *Kingfisher*."

"Ah," the captain said, perking up, "hide in plain sight. Is that the angle?"

"Repaint the name?" Cankelton said. "How am I supposed to repaint the name when we're in the middle of the ocean?"

The captain rubbed his chin. "Ropes," he said. "We'll dangle you over the side."

"Dangle me over the side," Cankelton cried. "What if I fall in?"

"We'll put you in a life jacket," Charlie said.

"I'll throw out the sea anchors so that we're moving along slowly. If you fall in, I'll haul you out lickety-split," the captain said.

"I'm coming down with bubonic plague from a rat bite," Cankelton said. "So it's not a great time."

"My good man," the captain said, "the only rat on this boat is you. You've been a phantom for the past ten years. Hanging over the side of the boat for an hour is the least you can do."

"Say we get clear of the Turks and Caicos," Charlie said. "Where were we supposed to go next?"

"The DR," the captain said, "also known as the Dominican Republic."

"And Manthi and Flynn might look for us there," Charlie said.

"Dang it," the captain said. "That's where the whole scheme falls apart."

"But they won't find us!" Charlie cried. "I'm pretty sure they found us this time by checking with different immigration offices to see if a boat named *Aladdin's Dream* came in. They had to have some kind of lead because, as you said, Turks and Caicos was off your usual route. They were probably checking all over the place. If I'm right, they'll keep checking with different immigration offices to see where you go next, and it will be nowhere."

"I get what you're saying," Gunter said to Charlie. "It will be as if the boat has disappeared into thin air because they'll be looking for the wrong name."

"They'll never figure out what happened," Charlie said. "I mean, they can't be very experienced at this kind of operation. How many people could they have possibly chased across the Caribbean Sea?"

"Probably more people than you would think," the captain said. "I'll tell you what, kid, you get Manthi and Flynn off my back and you've got free trips for life. That's what I think our chances are. I'll repaint the name to buy some time, but it's the kind of time that's gonna run out pretty quick."

Charlie's knees buckled. He gripped the side of the sofa to stop himself from falling to the floor. Did the captain just say free vacations? Free vacations? Every year? Free?

The odds of Charlie's dad paying for another vacation were slim to none. But free vacations? That was a concept Mr. Pennypacker could really get behind. If Charlie pulled this off, he could go on vacation every single year.

"Careful throwing around the word *free* near a Penny-packer," Gunter said.

Charlie stuck his hand out to the captain. "Deal."

. . .

The next hours were spent planning and preparing for the boat's name change. Charlie found cans of marine paint, brushes, and rollers in the storeroom. Cankelton had crept in to try to hide them, and then crept back out again when he saw they had already been found.

At dusk, they would use a roller with a long handle to erase "*Aladdin's Dream*" and "Wisney Cruises" with the same white color as the hull. At midnight, after the paint had dried, they would lower Cankelton down to paint on "*Kingfisher*" in dark blue. All the while, they would have to hide what they were doing from everybody else.

Late in the afternoon, the captain came over the loud-speaker. "Good afternoon, Wisney Cruisers! I've just had an urgent message from the National Weather Service and it seems we'll hit a patch of rough weather after sunset. Do not be alarmed! This captain has taken his old girl through hurricanes, tsunamis, ice floes, water spouts, algae blooms, pods of killer whales, and surprise tides! All passengers are to make their way below deck after six P.M. and remain there until morning while I fight off the weather. I will be watching the sea with hawkish eagle eyes; therefore, any lights one might view from their porthole is simply me watching the sea with hawkish eagle eyes and a flashlight. Sea anchors will be out, so expect to feel a slowing down of forward motion. Enjoy the rest of your day!"

Charlie and Gunter stood on deck at a railing, having hidden all the supplies behind a bulkhead.

"Are you sure we can really pull this off?" Gunter said, staring out to sea.

"I hope so," Charlie said. "Though a lot depends on Cankelton, and he doesn't exactly have nerves of steel."

"Well, we're not in danger of being murdered, like we thought," Gunter said. "So, I guess the agreement is null and void."

Charlie paused. He hadn't thought about that. He should be happy that he and Gunter Hwang could finally go their separate ways, but somehow he wasn't.

"*Technically* our lives aren't in danger anymore. But if we're serious about outfoxing a couple of Disney lawyers, covert operations will have to continue," Charlie said. "I could always add a rider that covers it."

Gunter glanced at Charlie. "Yeah," he said. "Riders are good."

. . .

Charlie found it hard to concentrate over dinner. Gunter was with the captain on the bridge, reviewing the plan to change the boat's name, which is exactly where Charlie should have been. He'd been on his way when his mom caught him in the corridor and insisted he take Olive in to dinner. If that weren't aggravating enough, Olive had been making comments about the conch farm dustup and ensuing parent/child conference ever since they sat down.

"Mommy said I can't tell people that I will fry them like a French fry ever, ever again. She said it was mean and hurtful."

"Good," Charlie said, pushing around his egg-and-sausage casserole.

"Now I'm gonna say 'boiling water,'" she said, looking pleased that she had found a loophole in her most recent contract. "Anybody against me has to go in boiling water. Like spaghetti."

"Mom didn't mean that you should think up another way to cook people."

"Spa-ghet-ti," Olive said quietly.

Charlie didn't answer, though he wondered how all this cooking of people was going to go over in first grade.

"I will be fair. I won't put them in boiling water if they do what I say," Olive said.

"And that's the problem," Charlie said, losing his patience. "The whole world is not going to do what one six-year-old says. Wait until you go to school. Who do you think will be in charge there? You? Some witch in your imagination? Or your teacher?"

Olive stared at him, then she burst into tears.

Charlie bit his lip. He leaned over and said, "Stop crying before mom sees you."

Olive hiccuped and sniffled. "I want it back the same," she whispered.

"Want what the same?" Charlie asked.

"Everything!" Olive said, spraying a fine mist of spit over his eggs. "I don't get carried anymore because I'm too heavy. I have to go to first grade and get a new teacher even though Mrs. Peach from my kindergarten loves me so much. I'm supposed to pick up my toys and it's so boring! Holding my breath doesn't work every single time any-more—I think they know that sometimes I'm breathing through my nose. I want everything back like it was."

Charlie stared at his sister. He suddenly realized what all the witch stuff was really about. She had settled into being the baby of the family and wanted to hold on to all the perks. She didn't want anything to change and she didn't want the responsibility that came with getting older. She didn't feel in control of anything anymore so she invented a powerful witch in her command.

"That's not how the world works," he said. "Things are always changing and you'll get more responsibility every year. Look on the bright side—one of these days you'll be old enough to buy your own toys. Then there won't be any more American Girl mix-ups."

Olive wiped her eyes and considered this aspect of getting older. "I do got a lot of quarters saved up."

"Yeah," Charlie said. "*My* quarters. Listen, if you want to make it in the first grade, you've got to stop stealing quarters and stop threatening people. Trust me, I've been there. You're about to move into the big leagues."

"Tell me how to make it in first grade," Olive whispered, the look of desperation written all over her face.

"It's pretty simple," Charlie said, "though it's gonna take some practice on your part so you better start now. Listen when other people are talking, say something nice about them, be helpful, and follow directions. If you do all that, you should be fine."

Olive wiped her nose on her sleeve and counted on her fingers, "Listen, nice, helpful, follow. That's like the kind of stuff Mrs. Peach says. Does it really work?"

"Of course it works," Charlie said. "That's why she told you to do it."

Olive stood up with a look of determination and marched over to Cinderalla smoking at the porthole. "I like your hair. Do you want my mommy to braid it for you? Do you want to talk about your hair while I listen? Do you have any instructions about your hair that I should follow?"

Cinderalla did not appear to recognize this transformation of Olive Pennypacker, but Charlie did. Fingers crossed that it would hold for more than five minutes.

· · ·

The sun had just dropped below the horizon and the sky had gone from dusk to dark. Mr. and Mrs. Pennypacker were safely ensconced in their cabin becoming acquainted with the new Olive Pennypacker. Charlie had left them as Olive told Mr. Pennypacker that he had pretty hair and asked him if he wanted to talk about it while she listened. Mr. Pennypacker, unlike everybody else who had been asked to talk about their hair, actually did have a few things to say about it. He had lectured his daughter on the cheap prices found at his barbershop compared to the highway robbery of Mrs. Pennypacker's salon and how the average Joe was an idiot to spend more than ten dollars on a haircut and how it was all a total rip-off anyway because you could cut your hair all day long and it would just grow back. At that point, Olive came to the end of her listening skills. She shouted, "Where are the hundred lost Dalmatians?"

Charlie figured Olive had a pretty realistic chance of getting through the first grade by complimenting everybody's hair and asking them if they wanted to talk about it. As long as they didn't actually want to talk about it.

Chapter Fifteen

Captain Wisner had brought all the supplies on deck. Cankelton brooded in his sanctuary, as he was not needed for this part of the mission. "I'd worry that he'd go missing," the captain said, "except now I know he's always holed up in his groovy man cave."

Charlie used a screwdriver to pry the top off a can of white paint. "Did you really have no idea what he did or where he slept?"

"None," the captain said. "There were times I thought he didn't even go on the trip. Like maybe he slipped off the boat before we left and slipped back on when we got back. I called him the 'useless phantom.'"

The captain shrugged. "Family. What are you gonna do? My sister spent thirteen hours in Vegas drinking mai tais and then married her bartender at a drive-through wedding chapel, now I got to pay the price."

Charlie had to agree with Captain Wisner's idea about family. You might wish you got a dad who was a big spender, but you got what you got. And anyway, except for the whole money-hoarding problem and Olive's plans to cook everybody, his family was pretty okay.

The captain screwed on the extension arm of the paint roller. Charlie poured white paint into the tray, and Gunter pointed the flashlight over the side. As the captain rolled the paint over "Wisney Cruises" and "Aladdin's Dream," he said, "I really thought this idea would take off. I mean, who doesn't like Disney?"

"Everybody likes Disney," Charlie said. "That's why the lawyers are after you. Not only would they not want anybody to steal their characters, but your version has to have them out of their minds. What Disney princess smokes Marlboros? Mickey Mouser has red hair and only knows how to cook eggs. Minnie Mouser isn't even here because she moved into the House of Pancakes. Cankelton hides out in a weird and disturbing lair and his costume is creepy—not exactly the charming and witty Jiminy Cricket we all know and love."

"These crew were the only people I could talk into it.

Brad and Clarissa both threw their notice at me the minute I mentioned Mickey Mouser and Cinderalla. But hang it, I watched those Disney ships with their thousands of paying passengers leave the docks a hundred times," the captain said. "All the while, I was losing my shirt on fishing trips. It seemed like a no-brainer—the Disney game was working for them, so it should work for me. Now, I'll have to sell up and get a job at Walmart."

Charlie was not so sure Captain Wisner would make a successful Walmart associate. He could just imagine some poor shopper asking where to find paper towels and being told the depth of the nearest body of water and what kind of sharks were in it. Still, he could see how the captain had been lured by the idea of patching up his finances with beloved Disney characters.

"You should've asked for advice from your regular customers," Gunter said. "I could have told you it was a bad idea."

"All right, you've both told me enough times already what a bad idea it actually was." The captain rolled over the last bit of blue paint. "That should do it."

"Now all we have to do is let it dry and repaint the name," Charlie said.

"All we have to do?" The captain staggered backward, like Charlie had said all they had to do was set the boat on fire. "Have you gone mad?" he asked. "Just change the name without appealing to Poseidon and Neptune?"

The captain shook his head. "I keep forgetting you're a swabbie new to the seafaring game. You can't just go willy-nilly changing a boat's name. Not on my watch!"

Charlie glanced at Gunter, who was pressing the top of the paint can back in place. Gunter nodded. "Obviously, you've got to appeal to Poseidon and Neptune."

"Obviously?" Charlie said. He supposed this was one of the things he'd missed when he'd been forced to take Olive in to dinner.

"Son, we've got to take care of the rolls," Captain Wisner said. "Poseidon and Neptune keep careful lists of every boat on the sea. Now, how's it gonna be if they notice one is gone and start inquiring?"

"I don't know," Charlie said. "How would that be?"

"They'd unleash their wrath on us," Gunter said.

The captain nodded. "We'd be sinking to the bottom before you could say 'Bob's your uncle.'"

Charlie did not have an uncle named Bob, but he got the

idea. "What are we supposed to do to fix the rolls?" he asked. "We don't have to sacrifice anybody, do we? Because I realize Olive irritates people, but I just couldn't allow that."

"Hah!" the captain said. "If human sacrifices were required, she'd be the first one over the side—helped in by pretty much everybody. No, my boy, we've got to speak a language the gods can understand. I've already removed all other traces of *Aladdin's Dream*, which wasn't hard since I can't afford to print names on everything. You're not gonna find monogrammed life jackets on this boat! Now, I have this, see," he said, drawing a small metal rectangle from his shirt pocket, "and I've written *Aladdin's Dream* on it in soluble ink."

Captain Wisner took a piece of paper from his pants pocket and began to read:

"Oh mighty and great ruler of the seas and oceans, to whom all ships and we who venture upon your vast domain are required to pay homage, we implore you in your graciousness to expunge for all time from your records and recollection the name *Aladdin's Dream*, which has ceased to be an entity in your kingdom. As proof thereof, we submit this ingot bearing her name to be corrupted through your powers and forever be purged from the sea."

The captain threw the metal overboard. Charlie watched it swallowed up by the black water.

"In grateful acknowledgment of your munificence and dispensation," the captain continued, "we offer these libations to your majesty and your court. Hand me that bottle, Gunter."

Gunter jogged over to the bulkhead and brought back a bottle of Welch's sparkling grape juice. Charlie had assumed it was refreshment for all their work, but apparently it was for Poseidon and Neptune.

The captain examined it and heaved a sigh. "It ought to be good champagne, but this is all we've got."

He twisted off the cap and poured it over the side from east to west. "Now we've done our duty. The gods are appeased, and we can ease them into going back to the *Kingfisher* later."

"Uh-oh," Charlie said. "Going *back* to the *Kingfisher*."

"What uh-oh?" the captain asked.

"Manthi and Flynn might already know that the boat used to be the *Kingfisher*," Gunter said. "Is that it?"

"That's it exactly," Charlie said. "Manthi and Flynn might already be checking for boats named *Aladdin's Dream* and *Kingfisher*. To really disappear, we need a totally new name."

"Blast it," the captain said. "I always miss one crucial

detail! It's just like the time I got on the Tower of Terror. I was approaching the big drop when I remembered I was afraid of heights. That realization was, as they say, too little too late."

"How about we rename her the *Octopus*?" Gunter said.

"Too many appendages for a boat," the captain said. "I'm thinking the *Barracuda*."

Charlie thought barracuda wasn't half bad, but an idea had occurred to him on how Captain Wisner might be able to salvage his business. If he was right, barracuda wasn't going to be the right name. "How about the *Captain Kidd*?"

Captain Wisner rubbed his chin. "Captain Kidd? A loyal captain unjustly treated by those with power? It sounds eerily like myself, if you ask me."

"Are you sure you don't want to go with the *Octopus*?" Gunter asked.

"The *Captain Kidd* it is," the captain said. "We meet back here at midnight."

. . .

Charlie had slipped below deck and silently entered his cabin. His mom and dad thought he'd been in there reading since after dinner. He'd already read most of the only book in his room—*A Bloody History of Caribbean Pirates*—so if they asked him about it he could recite some facts. He doubted he would be asked about it though; it sounded like they had their hands full with Olive.

It turned out that once she had expressed an interest in her father's hair, and then heard more about it than she wanted to know, Olive was done being considerate. There were complaints about the missing Dalmatians, complaints about the Dalmatian that was there, complaints about the eggs/baby birds situation, and finally, accusations about who stole Kooky Cookie, her favorite Shopkin. Mr. Pennypacker was singled out as the perpetrator of the crime, and as Olive did not believe in juries, she convicted him on the spot.

The hours ticked by, and Olive finally gave up threatening Mr. Pennypacker with jail time if Kooky wasn't returned unharmed and went to sleep. His parents talked quietly for another half hour and then all was quiet. Charlie waited another forty-five minutes until it was close to midnight. Time to dangle Cankelton over the side and turn this boat into the *Captain Kidd*.

• • •

The deck was eerily quiet. Charlie had grown used to the way it sounded during the day—the muffled noises of people talking below and Mickey Mouser banging pots and pans around in the galley. All aboard the boat were asleep except him, Gunter, the captain, and Cankelton.

Cankelton had shed his insect costume. He wore jeans and a thin white T-shirt tucked in tight. He looked smaller than ever—it was like the more layers you peeled back, the more he shrank. In a bathing suit, he was probably no bigger than one of Olive's Shopkins.

Cankelton's expression, upon being wrangled into a life jacket, was one that said he had known all along that his life would come to this sorry conclusion.

"Now, have a look at my handiwork," the captain said, holding up a rigged harness, "and tell me if this captain doesn't take care of his crew."

The seat of the harness was a boat cushion, the kind with a loop on either side. Charlie knew from Mickey Mouser's three-minute safety briefing that it was a flotation device. If a person found themselves in the water without a life jacket, that person should look around and hope a cushion floated by them. They could then grab the cushion and put their arms through the loops to stay afloat until the sharks got them.

(Mickey had not actually said anything about sharks—Charlie had gathered that particular fact from Olive's chumming expedition.)

Captain Wisner had run a long, thick rope underneath the cushion and knotted it on both of the loops. Some kind of seatbelt ran underneath the cushion and threaded through the loops.

"A weight belt to hold him in," Gunter said, looking over the contraption. "Good idea."

"Now," Captain Wisner said, "let's get a move on before old Cankelton faints on the spot."

Cankelton did, indeed, appear as if he might hit the deck. Charlie patted him on the shoulder. "You're going to be fine," he said. "Just think, your whole job tonight is to do something you're already good at. All those signs in your cabin were practice leading up to this."

Cankelton did not seem cheered by the idea that it was his moment to shine. He stared at the captain and whispered, "I'll tell my wife, your own sister, what you did to me."

The captain guffawed. "Right," he said. "Then she'd call me and scream, 'You had a chance to lose him at sea and you didn't take it?'"

The captain had run the loose ends of the rope to the other

Captain

side of the deck and threw them around cleats. "Gunter, Charlie, grab a rope each. You'll use the cleats as leverage. If you feel the rope slipping from your grasp, throw on a hitch knot double time."

"Slip?" Cankelton whispered. "Nobody said anything about slipping from grasps."

"Show me your hitch knots," the captain said.

Both Charlie and Gunter stood with the rope hanging limply in their hands.

The captain stared at their motionless ropes. He sighed and took Charlie's from him, expertly demonstrating a hitch knot. He made them practice it until they could do it fast enough to stop Cankelton from crashing into the sea. After a dozen tries, they were finally ready.

Charlie and Gunter grabbed hold of their ropes. The captain directed them to feed out the line until the seat

Kidding

cushion harness was just over the side.

"Ready, Cankelton? Remember, that's *Kidd* with two *d*s. Now, steady, boys." The captain picked up Cankelton like he was a toddler being put into a car seat. He dangled him over the side. "There you go," he said, cheerfully, "right into the harness like it was made for you. Which it was."

Charlie felt the rope tighten as Cankelton's weight settled into the harness.

"On my count," the captain said, "we lower him one foot at a time. Ready, one-two-three—lower."

Charlie nodded to Gunter and they slowly fed out the

ropes, using the cleats as leverage. They had to work together to lower the ropes at the same speed, otherwise, the seat cushion would be higher on one side and Cankelton would tip over.

"Now another foot," the captain said.

They lowered Cankelton, foot by foot, until the captain said, "Far enough. Tie off the cleats."

Charlie carefully tied his hitch knot, then slowly loosened his grip on the rope to be sure it would hold. Gunter did the same and they raced to the other side of the boat.

Charlie could just see the top of Cankelton's head below him, accompanied by soft whimpering. The captain threw a flashlight to Charlie and lowered down a bucket with the paint can and a brush, inch by inch, careful not to bang it against the hull. It landed in Cankelton's lap.

In the beginning, Cankelton's movements were sloth-like. He reached for the brush like he hoped his hand would never get there. But something took over when he first touched paint to the hull. It was as if he forgot all about dangling on a seat cushion, only held up by knots tied by two people who had just learned them. Cankelton was an artist, and his talent kicked in.

Cankelton began directing to be pulled to the right and left and lower and higher. He worked for over an hour and then gave the thumbs-up to be hauled back on board. After he tumbled over the rails, Charlie leaned out as far as he could and shined the flashlight along the hull. The lettering was expert and had a nice, old-timey flair. It was the name that came as a slight surprise.

Captain Kidding

Chapter Sixteen

Charlie really didn't want the captain to see the *Captain Kidding*. They had enough problems to deal with, and the *ing* could come off later. He was sure there was a lesson in there somewhere, like don't underestimate the smallest guy in the room, even if he's dressed as an insect and lives in a groovy man cave. If that insect cave-dweller wants to make a point about his unhappiness, he will find a way.

"It looks great," Charlie said, snapping the flashlight off. "And just in time, too; the batteries are dead."

. . .

The next morning, Charlie stared at his soft-boiled egg. The twins had picked theirs up, shook them, and then thrown them out a porthole. Claire had already cracked hers open, snapped a photo, and said, "Hashtag: not even cooking them now."

Olive sat down with toast. "I told Mickey, do not give me one more baby bird. Just do not."

The intercom crackled. The captain was about to make the announcement.

"Morning, morning, morning, folks!" the captain said. "And what a beautiful morning it is! Now, there is one little hiccup, but isn't there always? We had to burn through more fuel than expected last night, what with the rough seas and all, so we're gonna nip back into the Turks and Caicos, fill her up, and be on our way. No need to even get off the boat. We are in and then we are out. Meanwhile, enjoy Mickey Mouser's astounding cuisine!"

"It's astounding all right," Charlie said.

"What rough seas?" Olive asked, crunching on the toast she had demanded from Mickey Mouser.

"You probably slept through it," Charlie said.

"No I didn't," Olive said. "I was too scared to sleep. I can't ever sleep again until we get home. I'm gonna stay awake until we get home."

"Why?" Charlie asked. "Afraid somebody will creep in and kill all your Shopkins?"

"No," Olive said. "Somebody wants to creep in and kill *me*."

"Don't be so dramatic," Charlie said laughing. "Nobody is trying to kill you. They probably should be, but they're not."

"Oh yeah?" Olive asked, her voice dropping down to a whisper. "Last night, I saw a man outside my window."

Charlie gulped. Cankelton.

"He was a ghost," she continued. "A drowned ghost."

"Sounds like a bad dream," Charlie muttered.

Olive narrowed her eyes. "That's what mommy said when I woke her up and he was gone. Do you think that ghost is mad that I wanted to cook people? And also, for blaming daddy when I lost Kooky Cookie, and then I found Kooky under the bed this morning?"

"Would a ghost really care about lost Shopkins and stupid cooking threats? I highly doubt it," Charlie said, hoping to bring the conversation to a halt.

Gunter came to stand by Charlie. Charlie said, "My sister thinks she saw a ghost out her window last night. A ghost that wants to kill her." He stared at Gunter meaningfully, so he would get the hint that it had been Cankelton.

Gunter snorted and said, "That's what you get for threatening to cook people."

"I knew it!" Olive cried. "I'll never even make it to first grade!"

"Thanks, Gunter," Charlie said.

"You are very welcome. No more dawdling over this fine breakfast. The captain said he has something to show you on the bridge."

Charlie got up and reluctantly left his sister to repent her crimes and pray to the drowned ghost for forgiveness.

. . .

The captain leaned back in his chair on the bridge. "I saw the new name," he said. "The *Captain Kidding*. I ought to fire that brother-in-law of mine."

"He can fix it later," Charlie said.

"He *will* fix it later," the captain said. "Assuming I still have my boat. Otherwise, I'll end up as a Starbucks barista at the Miami airport, whipping up a grande, half-caf, half-sweet, coconut milk, cinnamon dolce latte for an idiot in a beanie who claims his name is Northeast Rainbow."

Charlie would have thought that description extreme, except there was a high school kid on his block who wore a beanie, carried around a Starbucks cup wherever he went, and was named Lobo Lupe Wolf. *Lobo* was Spanish for "wolf" and *lupe* was French for "wolf," so his actual name was Wolf Wolf Wolf.

"For now," the captain continued, "we'll be back at Turks and Caicos in twenty minutes. I'll dock her right at the fuel pumps and then I'll disguise myself and trot over to the immigration office with the passports."

"A disguise," Charlie said. "Good idea, planning for every contingency."

"What's your disguise?" Gunter asked.

"Tourist," the captain said. "I'll switch my captain's hat for a baseball cap pulled down low and put on a pair of dark sunglasses. I've got a T-shirt with a Turks and Caicos flag on it, then I'll add socks, sandals, and a fanny pack and voila—I blend right in."

"Genius," Charlie said.

"We should be out of there in under an hour," the captain said, handing Charlie and Gunter marine radios. "Keep an ear out in case we run into trouble. If you see anything happening around the boat, like Manthi and Flynn, radio me."

Charlie took his and looked at it. "Does it even work? You said you couldn't call the Coast Guard with them."

"It's a five-mile radius," the captain said. "Good luck finding the Coast Guard lollygagging around within five miles of you. Seems to me that wherever you are, they aren't. Now, you got to use proper marine radio protocol, mind. I got a reputation to uphold."

"There's a protocol?" Charlie asked.

"Obviously, there's a protocol," Gunter said.

"Do you know what it is?" Charlie asked him skeptically.

"I do not," Gunter said.

The captain sighed. "All right, swabbies, here's how it goes. You're on channel 16. Stay there and listen. If you need to call me, use the code name Big Dog. Press the button and say 'Big Dog, Big Dog, this is Kidd, over.' Just like that. Then take your finger off the button and listen. Don't—on no account—start talking on this channel. I'll say 'Kidd, this is Big Dog, switch.' Then we all switch to channel 68. You see how that's clever? Any nosy Parker listening in will know we're going to another channel, but he won't know which one. We'll be done talking by the time he figures it out."

Charlie nodded. It was a little bit more formal than the toy walkie-talkies he had used from his backyard to communicate with the Pennypacker kitchen. Those transmissions went something like, "Hey dad, we need more marshmallows out here." Then his dad would radio back, "There goes your college fund—too bad a doctorate in marshmallows won't get you a real job. Why are we living on Ramen noodles and air? Because we spent everything on marshmallows!" Then his mom would be in the background saying, "Charles, we are not rationing marshmallows on the Fourth of July."

They had docked at the marina and the attendant began fueling the boat. The captain came on deck, the brim of his baseball cap pulled down so low that Charlie wasn't sure how he could see. His outfit, down to the socks pulled up to his knees, really did make him look like one more tourist-dad who didn't care what he looked like. Charlie watched him stumble down the road and lurch into a taxi with his Ziploc bag filled with passports.

Charlie and Gunter had been ordered to stand at the bow and stern, keeping a lookout. Charlie was at the bow and had laid the marine radio down so he could look like he was casually enjoying the view instead of being on a mission. He scanned the marina for Manthi and Flynn, willing his stomach to stop flipping around. Nerves of steel were the most important part of executing any kind of daring plan. Except for his stomach, he felt like he was holding up pretty well.

He wondered if Gunter would tell everybody at school about the trip. And if Gunter would leave out the part where they thought the mob was after them. He figured Gunter had just as much skin in the game as he did, so he probably wouldn't highlight that unfortunate misunderstanding. The story would be all about racing across the Caribbean with mysterious men on their heels and the brilliant plan to outwit them.

He glanced at Gunter at the stern of the boat, also trying to look casual so that the parents who were sunbathing and trying to keep track of their kids at the same time wouldn't notice anything. Charlie wondered what his friend Kyle would do in this situation. He would probably do what Charlie told him to do. Usually, he really liked that Kyle let him make all the decisions and that Mrs. Kendreth thought all his decisions were brilliant, but in this situation, he was not so sure. If the captain did call on the radio, if there was some kind of trouble heading their way, he'd need a team ready to act boldly. The only team he had was Gunter, but at least he could be pretty sure that Gunter would act boldly. Usually stupidly, but always boldly.

The marine radio crackled to life. "Kidd, Kidd, this is Big Dog, over."

Charlie fumbled with the radio and pressed the button. "Big Dog, this is Kidd, over."

"This is Kidd, too, over," Gunter said.

"Switch, over," the captain said.

Charlie pressed the up arrow, scrolling through the channels to find 68.

"Big Dog, Big Dog, this is Kidd, over," Gunter said, looking triumphant that he had gotten to channel 68 first.

"The jig is up," the captain said. "The suits are here. They recognized me coming out of the immigration office."

"How?" Charlie asked. "How could they know it was you?"

"Um," the captain said through static, "I believe they may

have recognized my mid-section. At least, that's what they were staring at."

Charlie looked at Gunter. Manthi and Flynn had recognized the captain. They had been tipped off by that unmistakable belly. Round, like a taut beachball, it preceded the captain by at least half a foot. He should have known there was no disguising *that*.

"Is the boat refueled? Over," the captain radioed.

"The guy is near the shed, writing something down, over," Gunter said.

"That's the bill of sale," the captain said. "Go to the bridge. There's a credit card in a black pouch. Give it to him. We need to be ready to fly as soon as I get back. Over."

Charlie threw down the radio and raced to the bridge. He found the black pouch, grabbed the Visa card, and raced down the gangplank to the attendant. "The captain told me to give you this," Charlie said, nearly breathless.

The man nodded and took the card into the little shack on the dock.

Mrs. Pennypacker stood at the rails and called, "Charlie, what in the world are you doing?"

"Just paying for the fuel, mom," he called back.

Charlie heard a long screech of tires and stood on his toes to look toward the entrance to the marina.

The captain threw some cash at the driver and jogged toward the boat, holding the passports over his head.

Charlie waved him to the shack. "Over here, Cap!"

Captain Wisner's thin legs were pumping double time and his large belly bounced up and down. He grabbed the credit card receipt from the startled man, scribbled his name on it, and took his copy with the credit card. "All aboard, Charlie, not a moment to lose! I paid my driver extra to lose the bums, but they'll arrive in a matter of minutes."

They raced back to the boat and leapt on board. There was no sign of Cankelton, so Charlie ran to the bow and threw off the ropes. Gunter did the same at the stern. Jimmy Jenkins's mom propped herself on her elbows, looking around at the activity. "Wow," she said. "We're going already? That *was* fast."

The boat began to drift from its mooring as Captain Wisner ran up to the bridge.

Screeching tires on the gravel drive sprayed up dust in all directions. A second taxi had slammed to a halt in front of the marina. Charlie watched one of the lawyers wrestle his briefcase from the car while the other handed cash to the driver. They sprinted toward the dock.

The engines roared to life. The boat had drifted four feet from the dock by the time Manthi and Flynn reached it. Flynn, who Charlie now knew was the tall one who had flung himself into the sea the last time, grabbed a rope from the dock and threw it toward the boat. It sailed through the air and caught on a cleat. Flynn smiled and pulled it taut.

Chapter Seventeen

Flynn began to haul the boat in, while Manthi wrapped himself around Flynn to stop his partner from being pulled into the water. Charlie ran over and tried to unhook the rope, but it was too taut to budge.

The rope slacked for a moment as Flynn went hand over hand. Charlie wrenched it free and threw it off.

Flynn, now pulling on a rope attached to nothing, flew backward on top of Manthi. He rolled off his friend and yelled, "Young man, don't allow the captain to drag you into this!"

"Too late!" Charlie called.

"The new name doesn't fool us, Wisner," Manthi called, getting to his knees. "What's the point of running? We'll catch up to you eventually."

Captain Wisner leaned out the bridge's window and

shouted, "*Eventually* is not this minute and the *Captain Kidding* is now in international waters!"

"You're in Turks and Caicos' waters, as you well know!"

"Not for long," the captain shouted, pulling the boat ever farther from the dock. "We'll soon be in Bermudian waters!"

Charlie thought that was pretty clever. Pretending to let slip that they were going to Bermuda when they were really going to the Dominican Republic. Hopefully, Manthi and Flynn would be on the first flight going in the wrong direction.

The captain had gotten far enough from the dock to turn the boat seaward. They had fuel, stamped passports, and they'd escaped the lawyers once again. That was the good news. The bad news was that Manthi and Flynn were not at all fooled by the *Captain Kidding*. It was time for one last-ditch effort if Captain Wisner was going to save his boat.

Charlie's mom had watched the scene unfold on the dock. She stood with her arms crossed while other parents began to get up from their lounge chairs to see what was happening. Charlie knew that he was about ten seconds away from a courtroom interrogation. He dashed up to the bridge instead. Gunter was five seconds behind him. Gunter slammed the door shut and pulled down the shade.

"All the work we did was for nothing," Gunter said. "They weren't fooled by the new name at all."

"What now?" the captain said. "We're between a rock and a hard place, between an anvil and a hammer, between the devil and the deep blue sea."

"That's between a lot of things," Gunter said.

Charlie said, "Captain, you're giving up too easily. You can't just try one plan and then throw your hands up in defeat. You've got to switch to a plan B. We're going head-to-head with Disney lawyers; there were always going to be ups and downs."

"You have a plan B?" the captain asked.

"I think so," Charlie said. Then more firmly, "No. I know so."

Charlie had convinced the captain and Gunter that his idea would work. The captain had jumped on it immediately—he was like a drowning man grasping at a lifeguard's ring. Gunter had walked around the idea, poking it for holes and playing devil's advocate, aka being Gunter. His but-shouldn't-we's and what-ifs and I-doubts were annoying, but they helped refine the plan.

"It could work," Gunter admitted.

"It has to work," Charlie said.

"True," Gunter admitted. "Unless you have a plan C."

"I do not," Charlie said. "You?"

"Nope."

Charlie spent the next hour walking the crew through his epic plan B. Cinderalla blew smoke rings over Charlie's head and then burned a few holes in her gown for good measure. Mickey Mouser tore off his mouse ears, stomped on them, and ground them into the deck. Cankelton ripped off his Timiny Cricket costume and tried to throw it overboard, but the captain caught it before it went over the side. Whatever the crew really thought about the plan, they were wildly enthusiastic about getting rid of the Disney-like costumes.

Now it was time to introduce the concept to the boat's paying passengers. It was late afternoon, the time of day when the breeze died down and the color of the sea deepened from turquoise to gray-blue.

Charlie thought they could not launch the plan too soon. When he'd come down from the bridge earlier, his mom had tried to interrogate him. He'd claimed he didn't know anything about the men in suits and he'd just helped the captain fuel up the boat because he thought it would be fun. She had narrowed her eyes and chewed on her Trident gum, but he had not cracked. That, Charlie knew, was only a temporary win;

his mom would fire questions at him when he least expected it, until he finally spilled his guts. It would be just like the case of the missing dress slacks (he had ripped one of the knees and thrown them out), the mysterious disappearance of a box of Ring Dings (he had only meant to eat one, but then kept going back), and, most recently, the inexplicable C in math last year (he'd paid too much attention to Mrs. Carson's therapy dog and not enough to Mrs. Carson).

The rest of the passengers were just as suspicious as his mom. After racing out of the Turks and Caicos, the boat had become a hotbed of rumors. Every time Charlie passed somebody, he heard a new theory launched. Among the more interesting ideas that were being traded like baseball cards: The captain was wanted by the Feds for high crimes and misdemeanors. The captain, himself, had staged the military coup at Eleuthera. The captain was a drug lord kingpin posing as an inept boat captain. It was generally agreed that the captain had taken them out to sea again so they couldn't get cell service to call the authorities. The idea of a mutiny was bandied about, until it was realized that nobody knew how to drive the boat or what direction to drive it if they figured it out. Charlie's dad had a pad of paper and was making a list of all the reasons he could sue.

"Settle down, folks," the captain yelled over the swirling rumors, innuendos, accusations, and insinuations.

"Thank you," the captain said. "Now, I'd just like to say that it's perfectly natural to experience a few bumps in the road. That's what we've had here—bumps. Nothing more than bumps. The good news? It is all smooth sailing from here on in. Not a bump on the horizon as far as the eye can see. And for the record, I am not wanted for high crimes, I'm not a drug lord or planner of coups, and don't bother suing me because there's nothing to get. So there you have it— bumps in the road, all smoothed out."

"What are you talking about?" Jimmy Jenkins's mom asked.

"Yeah, what is he trying to say?"

"Whatever he's trying to say, I don't buy it."

"'Bumps in the road' goes right into the lawsuit," Mr. Pennypacker said.

"Hashtag: what the heck are bumps?" Claire muttered.

Mrs. Pennypacker stepped forward. "Folks, what we have here is a tap dancer," she said. "A song and dance man. I've seen defendants try the same thing a hundred times—they just keep talking fast and saying nothing. They hope you lose track of the point."

The captain backed away from Mrs. Pennypacker. Charlie realized that with all the talk of bumps and smooth sailing, the captain had told them nothing. He had to take over before a real mutiny got under way or, worse, his mom demolished the defendant. He decided he'd better lay out the cold, hard facts.

Charlie climbed the steps that led to the bridge and said, "Hold on,

everybody. The captain hasn't explained it right. Or explained anything, really. But I will."

Everyone quieted down. Except for Mr. Pennypacker, who waved his sheet of paper and said, "Just look at how long this list is!"

"Dad."

"Okay, okay. I'll show it to you later," Mr. Pennypacker said.

"First," Charlie continued, "we've all noticed that something is not exactly right on this boat. In fact, pretty much everything is not right. Number one: this Disney-like cruise is terrible. The characters aren't good, they don't enjoy their jobs, there's no waterslide, and we have had way too many eggs."

"Eggs are my jam," Mickey Mouser said, shoving his hands into his pockets. "People love my eggs."

There were various no-we-don'ts muttered and Olive shouted, "Baby bird killer!"

Charlie waved the crowd back to silence.

"What I'm saying is that even if a Disney-like cruise was ever going to be a good idea, which it never was," Charlie said, "the execution is lacking."

"I'll say it's lacking."

"Lacking is an understatement."

"Another thing for the lawsuit! Execution is lacking!"

"And number two, you have nobody to blame but yourselves," Charlie said.

"Excuse me?" Mrs. Jenkins said.

"We haven't done anything wrong!" Mr. Jenkins said, putting an arm around his wife's shoulders.

"Why can't we blame the captain?" the twins' mom asked.

"Because," Charlie said, ready to deliver the final blow, "you were the ones who decided to go on the cheap. You were the ones who decided not to go on a real Disney cruise. You sold out your kids' childhood dream vacation to save a couple of bucks."

Charlie had expected various arguments about how they

couldn't have known it would be so bad or that they kept an eye on value so their kids could go to college or that they'd thought it was a real Disney cruise and had been totally tricked. Instead, nobody said a word. Not even Mr. Pennypacker, who was diligently avoiding his wife's eye.

"Which brings me to number three," Charlie continued. "Those men in suits are Manthi and Flynn. They're Disney lawyers. Manthi and Flynn don't appreciate Disney-like cruises and the people who go on them. They might as well be Jafar and Maleficent. They will chase us to the ends of the earth. And don't think the captain is the only one on the hook. You are all accessories to his crime. If the captain goes down, so do you."

"When you say 'go down,'" Mr. Pennypacker said, "would you be referring to any kind of civil judgment that might demand a person's hard-won cash?"

"That's what I'm referring to, Dad."

Mr. Pennypacker staggered and his wife had to hold him upright.

Now that Charlie had brought them low, it was time to lift them up.

"But all is not lost!" he said. "We can still salvage this cruise and help ourselves out of the trouble we've gotten ourselves into. We've got to turn this boat from Disney-like to pirate-like before we dock at the DR—which is Dominican Republic for all you landlubbers. We've got to erase this Disney-like idea from the face of the earth so that those lawyers can't drag us all in front of a judge. Here's the plan."

Chapter Eighteen

Charlie laid out what everybody had to do. Olive protested against painting over her Dalmatian, until Charlie pointed out that she had been complaining about it the whole time. Cinderalla commented that she really would turn into Cinderella with all the sewing she had to do. The twins mainly complained in Cucuchara, so Charlie didn't know the details, but it involved a lot of pointing at him.

Mr. Pennypacker was not initially enthusiastic about helping the captain. He was too busy writing a list about why none of it was his fault, which he planned to submit in court. Charlie sat down next to him and said, "The captain promised that if we can get him out of this mess, we can have free vacations for life. Free, Dad. As in, no money to be paid."

"That kind of free?" Mr. Pennypacker said, looking intrigued.

"You know as well as I do that mom is never going to let you return to the backyard vacations. She's going to be planning actual vacations from now on."

Mr. Pennypacker paled. "It'll be the salon all over again. She goes once to get her hair done for our class reunion and all of the sudden it's every six weeks for the rest of our lives!"

"So the choice is fix the captain's problems and get free vacations for life, or don't fix them and pay cold, hard cash for vacations for life," Charlie said. "Of course, that's assuming the Disney lawyers have left you with any cold, hard cash. It's up to you, Dad."

Mr. Pennypacker considered watching cold, hard cash slip through his fingers. "Well, no use just standing around, then. There are deductions to be discovered, loopholes to slip through, offshore accounts to set up, dummy corporations to form! The sky's the limit!"

Charlie watched with satisfaction as Mr. Pennypacker dashed out the door. The captain's books were about to be massaged, examined with a microscope, raked over the coals, and square danced into a dizzying array of deduction dodges and tax weaves. Let the government keep up as best they could.

Long into the night, Mr. Pennypacker shouted various news from the bridge.

"Hold the French toast! The man has never itemized his taxes!"

"He's never heard of depreciation—somebody pound on my chest to restart my heart!"

"Good gravy! He spent thousands on this boat and not a receipt to be found!"

According to Mr. Pennypacker, the captain's problems were twofold: he didn't bring enough money in, but more importantly, he didn't do a good job keeping it out of the government's hands. When it came to taxes, Captain Wisner was a freewheeling Santa Claus. What the captain should have been was Ebenezer Scrooge—a skinflint skating to the edge of every deduction.

Charlie checked on Cinderalla in the dining hall. She had gathered together all the needles and thread meant for repairing cushions and deck chairs, and she'd been shown into Cankelton's sanctuary to get the black velvet off his couch to make pirate costumes for the crew. So far, she had spent more time smoking than sewing. Charlie stood next to her at a port-hole and told her about the pirate Mary Read and her daring exploits and proposed that Cinderalla was much better suited to be an adventurer than a princess. She appeared unmoved, until he mentioned that nobody had ever made a pirate lead a snorkeling trip. Cinderalla threw her cigarette out the port-hole and got to work.

Charlie helpfully left out the part where Mary Read died of fever in prison. Pirating might seem glamorous from afar, but when you read about their actual lives you realized that they pretty much always came to a pathetic end.

The twins were at another table, painting a strongbox with a skull and crossbones. From here on out, the captain would bury a treasure somewhere on the last island of the cruise for his passengers to find, using the clues and maps they had been working on since the first day. All the other islands would have clues hidden on them that would be necessary to track down along the way. The chest would hold the booty—a hundred dollars in nickels. They were silver, and two thousand of them would look like a really big haul.

The whole cruise would be one long treasure hunt, and the guests would live like real pirates. That part was cru-cial for the galley—the chef could serve hardtack biscuits and beef jerky all day long and nobody could really complain about it. Then, when they got an egg casserole, they would be grateful.

Olive had commandeered another table and had cornered poor little Jimmy Jenkins. She had asked him if he wanted to talk about his hair, but when he hadn't had anything interesting to say about it she'd run out of patience. He shrank smaller and smaller into his chair while she told him that she was a pirate and ordered him to get married or walk the plank. And that was an order. Also, they were going to find the pirate treasure together and be rich because that was her dream. Mrs. Pennypacker appeared to view this exchange as adorable until she noticed that Jimmy was weeping.

Charlie briefly spotted Cankelton as he raced past the door clutching his hair. His sanctuary had been opened up as a lounge for the guests. Mrs. Pennypacker and Jimmy Jenkins's mom had gone in there and spruced it up. The signs were down, the shag rug had been rolled up, and it turned out that under the black velvet of the sofa was a nice chintz. It had gone from 1960s dungeon to *the* place to be.

Claire acted as a model for Cinderalla. She spun around in a billowy skirt, snapped a selfie, and said, "Hashtag: pretty pirate."

Cinderalla held Claire still while she worked on the hem and muttered, "Hashtag: you get on my nerves."

Gunter came in to the mess hall. "Every cabin and door has been painted over. All the pictures in frames have been removed and been obliterated in the trash compactor. There's not a trace of Disney left on this boat."

"Perfect," Charlie said, examining the twins' handiwork on the strongbox.

"But what exactly are we supposed to do when Manthi and Flynn catch up to us? They're not stupid, you know. It will be obvious what we did and they can just tell a judge all about what they saw before we changed it from Disney-like to a pirate ship. They probably even have photos."

"Don't worry," Charlie said. "I have a secret weapon. I'll launch it when the time comes."

Though Charlie had a secret weapon to defeat Manthi and Flynn, he didn't want to say what it was. He thought the element of surprise would be crucial—not even the secret weapon knew it was a secret weapon.

"Maybe I have my own secret weapon," Gunter said.

"Okay, good."

"It's a secret."

"I totally get that."

Gunter spent the rest of the evening trying to figure out Charlie's secret weapon. As it happened, the secret weapon was hiding in plain sight.

. . .

At ten the next morning, the *Captain Kidding* tied up at the marina at Luperón, Dominican Republic. When Manthi and Flynn eventually turned up, and Charlie knew they would, they'd be faced with a boat that looked nothing like they remembered. He wasn't under any illusion that the lawyers would give up easily and go away, but Charlie was ready for the fight.

The captain hoisted a flag and radioed in to immigration and customs. Charlie and Gunter casually took up their posts at bow and stern, keeping an eye out for Manthi and Flynn.

Señor Morales, the official who boarded the boat to check the passports and confirm that the captain was not a smuggler of goods, stared at the captain's dazed passengers arranged across the deck. Mr. Pennypacker was draped over a deck chair, softly whispering about accrual basis versus cash basis. The twins were having a disagreement in Cucuchara that had descended into hair pulling, which might not have been so unusual except they were each pulling their own hair.

Jimmy Jenkins ran to Señor Morales and hid behind his legs. Olive dragged Mrs. Pennypacker by the hand, shouting, "Where is he? I just saw him!" Mickey Mouser came up from below and said loudly, "Don't pretend you don't know breakfast is ready. It's been ready for two hours and, that's right, it's eggs." Claire caught Señor Morales's eye, waved her arm across the deck, and said, "Hashtag: no sleep."

Señor Morales turned to the captain. "What is going on?"

Ten minutes later, Señor Morales had been informed of how deep the ocean was at various points in their journey, how low the pay was for the Coast Guard, how the captain wouldn't stand for cholera or military coups as a matter of principal, the fact that the chances of the immigration official being attacked by a shark were extremely low, and a description of the new pirate adventure the captain was planning.

Señor Morales hurried to complete the paperwork, shook Jimmy Jenkins off his leg, and jumped down to the dock. The captain grabbed a backpack and followed him off the boat to bury the treasure. Charlie watched Señor Morales break into a run to avoid having another conversation with the captain.

The captain was back from hiding the treasure within a half hour. Charlie thought that was a clue in and of itself. He'd seen the captain attempt to jog at Turks and Caicos and was sure he couldn't keep that sort of thing going for long. That meant the treasure could not be too far away.

That was a good thing—Charlie wanted to stay in the vicinity of the boat so he could spot Manthi and Flynn when they arrived. If the timing worked out the way he hoped, Charlie could find the treasure and then be kicking back with his one hundred dollars when the lawyers tried to board.

The loudspeaker crackled. "Ahoy, mateys! And notice I address you as 'mateys,' now that you are pirates! And *ahoy* means 'hello'! All hands on deck as we commence our exciting adventure into the world of pirating! Buccaneers—meaning crew—get thee below and heave ho yourselves into your costumes! Captain Kidd's Authentic Pirate Experience is set to launch! Thar she blows and over and out."

. . .

Ten minutes later, the captain came on deck dressed in a long, black velvet coat and breeches and a white shirt with a necktie long enough to be a scarf. His boat shoes were the only thing that didn't match up, but that could be fixed some other day.

Cinderalla, now known as Mary Read, had sewn herself

a full skirt of white sheets and a black velvet tight-fitting top. She had found a pipe somewhere, and now she smoked a cigarette with her right hand and the pipe with her left hand. She was a hazy figure, enveloped in smoke, as if she were a ghost pirate.

Mickey Mouser, now forever known as Kill Devil Ned, wore a white shirt with billowing sleeves, black pantaloons, and a broad black sash. He defiantly ate from a plate of scrambled eggs.

Since they'd run out of the black velvet material, Cankelton's only costume was a black eye patch and a black bandanna tied around his head. He looked even shiftier than usual with just one eye showing.

"Ahoy, mateys," the captain said to the passengers gathered around him, "which I already said means 'hello.' This old sea dog has the clue to the pirate's booty. Shiver me timbers, am I right?"

Charlie glanced down the pier. Manthi and Flynn were nowhere in sight. Looking around the deck, he couldn't say that anybody's timbers were shivering, but at least everybody looked interested.

"Now, pirates," the captain said, "I will post the clue right here on the bulkhead. Whoever finds the treasure chest will find a one-hundred-dollar IOU inside, as I haven't had time to get my hands on two thousand nickels and I don't, at this very moment, have a hundred dollars to pay for two thousand nickels. Yo ho ho, right?"

"Oh, he's learning and learning fast," Mr. Pennypacker said, rubbing his hands together. "Every passenger on this boat should be demanding a full refund, and instead he's making them fight for a hundred dollars. And it's not even cash, it's an IOU. A stroke of genius."

Charlie raced to the bulkhead. The sheet of paper the captain had taped to it said:

> Pirates seek refuge from storms at sea
> Hiding in coves is where they'll be
> A lair to lay low
> An oasis to go
> A calm haven of serenity.

"A limerick?" Gunter asked, coming up behind him.

The twins were pointing and speaking in rapid Cucuchara.

Claire snapped a selfie and said, "Hashtag: find me some money."

Mrs. Pennypacker held Olive up and read the limerick to her. Olive wriggled out of her mother's arms. "It's too hard!" She marched over to Jimmy Jenkins. "Figure it out so we can get married!"

Jimmy let out a howl like he was being mauled by dogs.

Mr. Pennypacker elbowed his way to the front of the crowd. "Make way," he said. "The Pennypackers are on the hunt for profit!"

Charlie reread the clue. It didn't say much. The only location it even mentioned was a cove. They were in a cove, but it was a pretty big place. Where were they supposed to start?

"Hey, Captain," Charlie said, "are you sure you put enough clues in there?"

The captain laid his index finger along his nose. "It's all there, Charlie."

Charlie read through it again. "Pirates seek refuge from storms at sea, Hiding in coves is where they'll be, A lair to lay low, An oasis to go, A calm haven of serenity."

"It could be anywhere in the cove," Gunter said. "We'll be digging for days."

"I know," Charlie said, "and that doesn't make sense."

"It's the only thing that makes sense," Gunter said. "We saw the captain leave with the booty, we know he wasn't gone long, so it has to be around this cove somewhere."

They both stared at the words. Charlie ignored the twins' screeching and Claire's hashtagging and Olive's dark threats to Jimmy Jenkins. *Cove* was not enough to go on. There had to be other meanings.

Hiding, lair, lay low, oasis, haven, serenity.

Hiding, lair, and *lay low* were similar. They were all places a person would go if they didn't want to be seen. *Oasis, haven,* and *serenity* were similar—a feeling of safety and comfort. So,

241

a comfortable place where nobody could see you? A safe lair? A comfortable place to lie low?

A comfortable place to lie low. Of course, that's what it was.

He knew what it meant. The treasure was in Cankelton's old sanctuary.

Charlie turned toward the steps.

"Oh, no," Gunter said.

"Oh, yes," Charlie answered, "I've figured it out."

"Manthi and Flynn," Gunter said.

Charlie turned. The lawyers were marching down the dock toward the boat.

What? Why now? Why did they have to show up now? The treasure was waiting for him downstairs. Somebody else might figure out the clue any minute.

Cankelton ran and pulled in the gangplank.

The lawyers were only a hundred yards away. The showdown couldn't happen without Charlie. He was the only one who knew about the secret weapon or would even know how to activate it. There was no time to get the booty.

But why shouldn't he get the hundred dollars? Why should he have to give up the treasure to deal with the captain's problems?

"Here we go," Gunter said.

Charlie was rooted to the spot. He knew what he should do: he should forget about the money and deal with Manthi and Flynn. But the pull of a hundred dollars all his own was like a magnet. He'd never had that much money! Knowing his dad, he'd *never* have that much money.

Charlie's mind was at war with itself, very much like it had been during the final Edge of the World tournament that he'd played with Gunter. That time, he knew what would be right, but he couldn't help doing the opposite anyway.

Chapter Nineteen

Charlie looked at the lawyers and then back at the staircase that led to the treasure. He was torn in two, just like he'd been that day in the cafeteria.

The year before, the whole school had played Edge of the World on their phones at lunch. There were regular tournaments to see who could flick their ship closest to the edge of the world without going over. There was an extra point for knocking an opponent's ship over the side. Charlie thought it was kind of boring, but Gunter was all in. Charlie played half-heartedly and let Gunter win. I mean, who cared?

Charlie always hid his smile when Gunter did his victory lap. The guy was not just a sore loser, he was a sore winner, too. Charlie could not have cared less. Until the day Gunter decided to raise the stakes.

"I bet you five dollars you can't beat me," Gunter said.

Five dollars? That was a whole week's allowance. "I don't want to play for money," he said.

"What's the matter, Pennypacker?" Gunter said, taunting. "Afraid you haven't packed away enough pennies?"

"I'm not being cheap," Charlie said. "I just think it's stupid to play for money."

"Scared, more like it," Gunter said. "Never mind, it wouldn't be a fair fight anyway, since I always win."

Charlie could feel his blood rushing in his ears. He had put up with Gunter's competitiveness since they met in first grade. He had been good-humored about it, reasoning that everybody's friend had some kind of flaw and this was just Gunter's. But now all these people were looking at him. He couldn't back out, and he wasn't going to give up five dollars just to make Gunter feel like a winner. He knew he should just let it slide, but he couldn't. Gunter had pushed him too far this time.

"You're on," Charlie said. "Let's play."

Everybody in the cafeteria had gathered round the table to see who would lose five dollars. Gunter took the first shot and sat back, looking supremely confident. Charlie leaned over the phone and carefully aimed. He flicked his ship and it sailed forward, knocking Gunter's right over the side and coming to rest at the edge.

Somebody shouted, "Pennypacker just got the first point plus a bonus point!"

Charlie smiled at Gunter. Then he delivered the final blow. "By the way, Hwang, I've been letting you win all year. You're not nearly as good as you think you are."

The crowd laughed and Gunter's face went beet red. Charlie got a sick feeling in his stomach. He should just stop this. Get up and walk away.

"Nice try, Pennypacker," Gunter said, taking in a deep breath and looking more determined than ever.

Charlie didn't get up and walk away, and the game went on, the two sides determined to destroy each other. It was close, but in the end, Charlie scored the final point. Gunter stood up and threw five dollars on the table while the whole school laughed at him. Charlie found out later that Gunter had gone home sick that day. He'd felt pretty sick himself, and the five dollars was still at the bottom of his sock drawer.

The next day, Gunter made a point of avoiding him on the bus. And so that was that. Charlie had thought of apologizing, but he hadn't. He was convinced that the only reason the whole thing even happened was because Gunter had pushed him too far.

Now, with the treasure so close and the lawyers marching toward the boat, Gunter eyed him. "You're kidding me. After all this, you're thinking about going after the money. That's a Pennypacker for you."

Stung by the comment, Charlie said, "Well, you're all about winning. That's a Hwang for you."

"Maybe," Gunter said.

"So?" Charlie said. "Aren't *you* going after the treasure? Don't you want to win?"

Gunter folded his arms. "No."

"Really?" Charlie asked.

"Really," Gunter said. "How about you?"

The lawyers were just feet from the boat. Charlie had come up with the whole plan. He'd figured out the secret weapon. Was he really going to ditch the whole idea for a hundred dollars? He'd always been waiting for Gunter to figure out there were more important things than winning. Maybe he ought to take his own advice and realize there were more important things than a stupid IOU for a hundred dollars. It had occurred to him more than once over the past year that he had wrecked a friendship over five dollars. That he might be becoming . . . his dad. He loved his dad, but he didn't want to go through life freaking out over five dollars.

Charlie turned to Gunter. "No. I'm not going after the treasure, either. Let's do this."

"Seriously?" Gunter asked.

"Dead serious."

Gunter smiled and said, "Okay, let's do this."

The lawyers had reached the boat. Flynn's right eye was black-and-blue, and he had a bandage on his nose from the last time he'd tried to board.

The captain glanced at the bridge as if he was ready to start the engines and head out to sea.

Charlie gave one last glance toward the stairs leading to the treasure, then he said, "Hold on, captain. This time we're not running to the next port. This time, we stand our ground. Prepare for battle. Just follow my lead."

Flynn launched himself onto the side of the boat and caught the railing. He hoisted himself over the top and landed on his head, then rolled like a ninja and leapt up. He stumbled back to the rail to give Manthi a hand. Once he had Manthi over, they collapsed in a heap on the deck.

The lawyers staggered to their feet, looking amazed that they had finally gotten on the boat.

"You have not been given permission to board," the captain said.

The lawyers glanced at each other. One of them said, "Michael Flynn, Esquire, Captain. And I would say that is the least of your problems."

"That's right, Captain," Manthi said.

"Why should I have any problems?" the captain asked. "As you can see, I'm running an innocent little pirate adventure tour here. Blimey, look at my crew of pirates!"

"But that's not what you *were* doing." Flynn said. "We saw you."

"That's right, we saw you. You were violating Disney's intellectual property."

"I can't comment on what you *think* you saw," the captain said. "After all, how would I know how much rum punch you've been drinking?"

"We haven't been drinking!"

"We even have pictures! Documented evidence."

"So you say," the captain said. "As you have declared yourself my enemy, I will send a representative to parlay. That's piratespeak for 'talk on my behalf.' Charlie?"

"Time for the secret weapon," Charlie whispered to Gunter.

Gunter looked around, like maybe there was a cannon hidden somewhere, but Charlie just sidled up to Olive. "Those people are from Disney. They know Minnie."

Charlie stepped back as Olive took in the information. Her face scrunched up, her eyes got a little watery. She ran to Flynn and threw her arms around his legs.

"You know Mickey and Minnie?" she whispered.

"Um," Flynn said, "not personally."

"You have to find Minnie and tell her they are not allowed to break up. They are not allowed! They have to be together forever and ever."

Flynn looked hopefully around the deck to see if somebody might remove the child clutching his legs. Mrs. Pennypacker folded her arms and chewed her Trident gum. Mr. Pennypacker shrugged, like Olive could belong to anybody.

"Hey, Olive," Charlie called, "they won't give your message to Minnie. All they want to do is take the treasure money. You know, the money you were going to use to get married."

If his calculations were correct, Charlie's little sister would, upon hearing this news, turn herself into a six-year-old atomic bomb. If ever a girl wanted to get married to an extremely reluctant bridegroom, it was

Olive Pennypacker.

Olive disentangled herself
from Flynn
and stepped
back so she

could stare into the two men's faces. "Treasure is my dream!" she shouted. "I need it to get married! Why? Why would you take my dream?"

Manthi shuffled his feet. Flynn mumbled, "I'm not saying we'll take all the money, but some compensation will be necessary. A judge will decide. You see, it's all about copyrights and trademarks and that sort of thing."

"Wow," Charlie said loudly. "Walt Disney crushes a six-year-old's dreams. I never saw that coming."

"What? No we didn't! We don't crush children's dreams!" Manthi cried. "We're just trying to serve papers on a lawsuit. The last thing we'd do is crush a dream!"

"We *make* dreams," Flynn confirmed, feeling around his scalp for the bump that was emerging on it from landing on his head. "We never crush them. Not ever."

"Are you sure?" Charlie asked, pointing at Olive. "Because that poor kindergartner looks pretty crushed. Look at that crushed little face."

Olive, Charlie knew, was a master at showing a crushed little face. Her lip curled and a single tear ran down her cheek.

Manthi turned to Flynn. "She's got a crushed little face! We can't allow Disney to crush faces! This is exactly the kind of thing that would make the news—Disney lawyers crush young girl's dreams. Who'd believe we didn't? People love six-year-olds and they hate lawyers! Do you ever see lawyers being adorable on YouTube? No, it's all six-year-olds! CNN, *Good Morning America*, *60 Minutes*—they'd be all over it. What are we going to do?"

Olive watched the men closely and Charlie guessed she was enjoying the effect she had on them. She took in a deep breath and delivered the knockout punch.

"My dreams are crushed!" Olive said, sobbing. "I didn't even make it to first grade and my dreams got crushed."

"No, no," Flynn said to Olive. "Your dreams are fine!" He ran over to the captain and said, "Tell her! Tell her that her dreams are fine!"

The captain clasped his hands behind his back, looking every inch the pirate. "Are her dreams fine, though? Could this sweet young lass assure herself that her boat won't be chased by lawyers from here on in? Could she sleep easy knowing that any papers in any lawyer's briefcases had gone up in a puff of smoke, never to be heard from again?"

Flynn appeared to be making calculations in his head.

Manthi whispered, "And what if Oprah got wind of it? The whole family would cry on television, then all of America would tweet and Facebook about it. There might even be a boycott. We'd be turned into the kind of villains Disney takes pride in defeating!"

The mention of Oprah Winfrey seemed to be the last straw for Flynn. He sighed and said to the captain, "If you promise that you'll stay a pirate ship. No more Disney-like cruising. That's the only way the papers disappear into a puff of smoke."

"Done," the captain said. "Now, there, young Olive, these nice men have decided to uncrush your dream."

"They uncrushed it?" Olive said, sniffling.

"Totally uncrushed," Manthi said hurriedly. "Dream away."

"I'll be rich and get married?" Olive asked softly.

"Sure," Flynn said. "Why not? Anything is possible. Give our regards to the lucky gentleman."

Olive skipped across the deck and said, "See, mommy? Sometimes yelling and crying *does* work. My dream got uncrushed."

Charlie stared at the lawyers. "Well? Don't you have any real criminals to chase around?"

Flynn sighed. "Of course we do. We always do. Our next case is in Omaha, Nebraska. We've heard there's a bakery there, moving a ton of Mickey Mouse cakes."

"And if one of those cakes makes somebody sick?" Manthi

said. "It's all Disney's fault, right? Don't you see what we're up against?"

"At least Children's World Bakery can't keep moving to another port," Flynn said.

"Before you go," Charlie said, "my mom will write up some paperwork about how you won't chase us around anymore and how papers went up in a puff of smoke. Just so we all understand each other."

Mrs. Pennypacker nodded. "Be warned, though," she said. "My agreements are notoriously ironclad. I didn't go to Harvard for the food."

Flynn cleared his throat. "Well, I don't know that we'd be authorized to actually sign anything."

Manthi said, "We'd need the greenlight from corporate if we were going to put something in writing."

"Dreams!" Olive shouted.

"All right, all right," Flynn said. "We'll sign."

"Follow me, gentlemen," Mrs. Pennypacker said.

As the lawyers passed by Olive, she whispered, "Like a French fry," but they were too frightened by her dreams to stop and ask what she meant.

They reached the top of the stairs and were nearly bowled over by the twins, racing up to the deck with the pirate's chest. They screeched in Cucuchara, while their mother called over them, "They found it!"

Mr. Pennypacker sank to the deck with his head in his hands. "So close to a hundred dollars in IOUs and it just slips through my fingers to the dolphin sisters!"

Charlie patted his dad's shoulder. It was a lot of money to lose, but he was glad he'd lost it.

"So," Gunter said to Charlie, "you didn't go after the money."

"No," Charlie said. "And you didn't go after winning."

"No," Gunter said.

"We should probably draw up a new agreement," Charlie said.

"What for?" Gunter asked.

"You know," Charlie said, hearing his voice stutter, "for going forward. If you want to go forward."

"Well," Gunter said. "It's not so much what I want, as what makes sense. In case we get chased by anybody else. Let it just be noted, though, that it was your idea to go forward. I could take it or leave it."

Charlie silently cursed Gunter Hwang. Hand the guy an olive branch and he'd just pull off all the olives and hit you over the head with the dead branch. He supposed somebody was going to have to be the bigger person and it wasn't going to be Gunter. Not that he'd tell Gunter that and start a whole new round of debate.

"Fine," Charlie said. "Let's get it done."

Charlie and Gunter made their way down to the dining hall. Before they reached the bottom of the stairs, they heard Flynn shouting. "What are you? Some kind of maniac?"

Charlie smiled. His mom was killing it at drawing up an ironclad agreement for the Disney lawyers.

They came into the room and found Mrs. Pennypacker laughing merrily. Manthi clutched his hair, and Flynn's eyes were watering.

"Hey, Mom," Charlie said, "can I borrow a piece of paper and a pen?"

Mrs. Pennypacker nodded and handed them over, but did not take her eyes off Manthi and Flynn. "Well, gentlemen, let's move on to the next clause, shall we?"

Manthi and Flynn leaned over and stared at Mrs. Pennypacker's pen racing across the paper, boxing them in tighter than cornered rats on a sinking ship.

Charlie sat down and wrote:

I, Charles J. Pennypacker Jr., do hereby agree to reestablish friendly relations with Gunter H. R. Hwang. Pennypacker commits to remembering that money is not the most important thing in the world (though pretty important and he still refuses to bet on stupid games).

Charlie slid the paper to Gunter. Gunter read it over and then wrote:

I, Gunter H. R. Hwang, do hereby allow myself to be talked into reestablishing friendly relations with Charles J. Pennypacker Jr. Hwang agrees to remember that winning is not the most important thing in the world (though definitely in the top two and this does not mean he has any plans to become a regular loser of games, contests, tournaments, or races).

Charlie read through it. Mrs. Pennypacker continued to badger Manthi and Flynn, out-lawyering the lawyers. Then, to follow her lead, Charlie and Gunter added a few lawyerly "herein" and "forthwith" flourishes to their agreement.

"We should sign it in blood," Gunter said.

Charlie sighed. Gunter Hwang always had to raise the stakes, no matter what it was. "You go ahead and slice your finger open," he said. "I'll use ketchup."

Charlie reached for the ketchup bottle at the end of the table, squirted a drop on the paper next to his name, and pressed his thumb on it. "Done."

Gunter seemed to consider his options. Deciding he'd rather not go get a knife from the galley, he said, "I concur that ketchup is now hereby recognized as a reasonable substitute for blood." He dribbled ketchup on his thumb and pressed down next to his name.

Gunter stared at his thumbprint. "Mine looks better, a definite win."

"Are you kidding me?" Charlie asked. "You just signed an agreement promising not to have to win everything."

"Right," Gunter said. "Starting now."

This was what the rest of his life was going to look

like—he'd do one thing, then Gunter Hwang would figure out a way to do it differently and claim victory.

. . .

The cruise back to Miami showed the *Captain Kidding* as a boat entirely changed. The new lounge was a big hit with the passengers, and they took to playing board games and charades in the evenings. Manthi and Flynn had stayed on the boat, exhausted after their conference with Mrs. Pennypacker and the ironclad agreement she had harangued them into signing. Fortunately, it turned out that Flynn was particularly talented at charades, even with a broken nose, black eye, and possible concussion. Manthi was obsessed with Monopoly, though he could be counted on to spend most of his time in jail and never seemed to realize that buying utilities would never pay off.

Cinderalla, now the fierce pirate Mary Read, surprised everybody by slinking in that first night, dressed in a sequined evening gown. She lay across the sofa and told everybody to imagine she was draped across a piano. She did a rousing rendition of that old Sinatra classic "My Way," which was both disturbing and strangely gripping.

Cankelton was given a small empty cabin as his own, and since the shag rug was too big for it, he just ran it up the walls. The lava lamp cast interesting shadows on the rug, and he said he really was as snug as a bug in a rug. The captain assigned him to permanent anchor watch. As Cankelton had remained firm in his hatred of guests and people in general, this was finally a job he could excel at.

Mrs. Pennypacker and Mrs. Jenkins went shopping in the DR, restocked the kitchen, and threw Kill Devil Ned out of it. Mr. Pennypacker was initially horrified that some of his hard-earned cash was going into other people's mouths, but he was soothed by the ensuing improvements in the galley. Eggs were out, and hamburgers, spaghetti, and copious amounts of cereal were in.

Olive remained unwilling to give up Jimmy Jenkins. The new plan, since they would not be as fabulously rich as she had hoped, was that Jimmy had to get a job and turn over all his money to his bride. She was going into first grade as an unrepentant gangster.

Charlie's agreement with Gunter held, and when he got back home he had to break the news to Kyle. Kyle was leery of befriending Gunter, especially since he had been under the impression that he was supposed to hate Gunter Hwang. Charlie had to explain that he might have exaggerated a few things, like when he said "Gunter Hwang is the devil's son and you should hate him." Kyle decided to be agreeable about the mix-up.

Gunter was never going to be a perfect friend—he was ornery and prickly, and even though he'd agreed that competition wasn't the most important thing, he had to be reminded all the time. Kyle *had* been a perfect friend, until Gunter got a hold of him. Gunter pointed out that the whole world didn't have to agree with everything Charlie Pennypacker said. Kyle caught on to that idea surprisingly fast.

Mr. and Mrs. Hwang were unhappy that Gunter had lost some of his competitive edge, Mr. Pennypacker was unhappy that Charlie had known where the treasure was and didn't go after it, and Mrs. Kendreth was unhappy that Kyle had suddenly developed a lot of strong opinions. All in all, Charlie figured they were probably all on the right track.

Captain Ignatius Wisner sent Charlie a few postcards. Kill Devil Ned's girlfriend had come back to work. He'd finally convinced her to see a doctor after she'd been caught eating pounds of bananas in a grocery store. It turned out she had been riddled with tapeworms. Monsters Inside Me did a whole show about her, and a prescription wiped them out. Now, she could go to a Chinese restaurant without making the chef cry.

Cinderalla, aka Mary Read, made an excellent pirate. Her weathered exterior, raspy voice, and habit of chain smoking suited the character. In the evenings, she transformed herself into a somewhat less excellent lounge singer. In between belting out Sinatra tunes, she liked to regale guests with the gruesome tale of the six-year-old heathen child who caused a blacktip reef shark attack.

The last postcard from the captain explained that his pirate trips had proved so popular that he'd been bought out by a corporation. Sadly, that corporation would not honor any oral agreements, like free trips for life, made by the captain.

Mr. Pennypacker was both distraught over losing something that was free and admiring of the rampant corporate greed.

Mrs. Pennypacker was more sanguine. She had already decided their next trip would be to Paris. Her husband, once apprised of this scheme, began to make lists of French things that could kill a person in a desperate bid to hold her off. He proposed that thousands of people fell down the Eiffel Tower stairs every year, as they were notoriously slippery with French butter, and that French people had sixteen different ways to say "I hate Americans," because they fervently hoped that Americans would stay in America.

Mrs. Pennypacker was undaunted by these dire warnings and carried her Pfeffernüsse cookie recipe and a pack of matches around in her pocket for the inevitable showdown.